R. Brimley Johnson, W. Cubitt Cooke

Popular British Ballads, Ancient and Modern

Vol. III

R. Brimley Johnson, W. Cubitt Cooke

Popular British Ballads, Ancient and Modern
Vol. III

ISBN/EAN: 9783744676960

Printed in Europe, USA, Canada, Australia, Japan

Cover: Foto ©Andreas Hilbeck / pixelio.de

More available books at **www.hansebooks.com**

Popular British Ballads

And like a ghost, through narrow passages
Walking, feeling the cold walls with her hands.

FAIR ELEANOR, p. 28.

POPULAR BRITISH BALLADS

ANCIENT AND MODERN

CHOSEN BY
R BRIMLEY JOHNSON
ILLUSTRATED BY
W CUBITT COOKE

IN FOUR VOLUMES
VOL. III

LONDON ❧ J. M. DENT & CO. Aldine House
69 Great Eastern Street E.C.
PHILADELPHIA ❧ J. B. LIPPINCOTT COMPANY
MDCCCXCIV

CONTENTS
VOL. III

he Contents ≈   ix

e Contents ≈

Note.—Since Vol. I. was printed, I have received Miss
Hawker's kind authorisation to include *The Doom-
Well of St Madron.*

LIST OF ILLVSTRATIONS

The Hermit

" Turn, gentle hermit of the dale,
    And guide my lonely way
To where yon taper cheers the vale
    With hospitable ray.

" For here forlorn and lost I tread,
    With fainting steps and slow,
Where wilds, immeasurably spread,
    Seem length'ning as I go."

" Forbear, my son," the hermit cries,
    " To tempt the dangerous gloom ;
For yonder faithless phantom flies
    To lure thee to thy doom.

"Here to the houseless child of want
  My door is open still;
And though my portion is but scant,
  I give it with good will.

"Then turn to-night, and freely share
  Whate'er my cell bestows;
My rushy couch and frugal fare,
  My blessing and repose.

"No flocks that range the valley free
  To slaughter I condemn;
Taught by that Power that pities me,
  I learn to pity them:

"But from the mountain's grassy side
  A guiltless feast I bring;
A scrip with herbs and fruits supplied,
  And water from the spring.

"Then, pilgrim, turn, thy cares forego;
  All earth-born cares are wrong:
Man wants but little here below,
  Nor wants that little long."

Soft as the dew from heaven descends,
  His gentle accents fell:
The modest stranger lowly bends,
  And follows to the cell.

Far in a wilderness obscure
   The lonely mansion lay—
A refuge to the neighbouring poor,
   And strangers led astray.

No stores beneath its humble thatch
   Required a master's care ;
The wicket, opening with a latch,
   Received the harmless pair.

And now, when busy crowds retire
   To take their evening rest,
The hermit trimmed his little fire,
   And cheered his pensive guest :

And spread his vegetable store,
   And gaily pressed and smiled ;
And, skilled in legendary lore,
   The ling'ring hours beguiled.

Around, in sympathetic mirth,
   Its tricks the kitten tries,
The cricket chirrups on the hearth,
   The crackling faggot flies.

But nothing could a charm impart
   To soothe the stranger's woe ;
For grief was heavy at his heart,
   And tears began to flow.

His rising cares the hermit spied,
  With answering care opprest :
And " Whence, unhappy youth," he cried,
  " The sorrows of thy breast ?

" From better habitations spurn'd,
  Reluctant dost thou rove ?
Or grieve for friendship unreturn'd,
  Or unregarded love ?

" Alas ! the joys that fortune brings,
  Are trifling, and decay ;
And those who prize the paltry things,
  More trifling still than they.

" And what is friendship but a name,
  A charm that lulls to sleep,
A shade that follows wealth or fame,
  But leaves the wretch to weep ?

" And love is still an emptier sound,
  The modern fair one's jest ;
On earth unseen, or only found
  To warm the turtle's nest.

" For shame, fond youth, thy sorrows hush,
  And spurn the sex," he said ;
But while he spoke, a rising blush
  His love-lorn guest betray'd.

Surprised he sees new beauties rise,
  Swift mantling to the view :
Like colours o'er the morning skies,
  As bright, as transient too.

The bashful look, the rising breast,
  Alternate spread alarms :
The lovely stranger stands confest
  A maid in all her charms.

And, " Ah ! forgive a stranger rude—
  A wretch forlorn," she cried ;
" Whose feet unhallow'd thus intrude
  Where Heaven and you reside.

" But let a maid thy pity share,
  Whom love has taught to stray ;
Who seeks for rest, but finds despair
  Companion of her way.

" My father lived beside the Tyne,
     A wealthy lord was he ;
And all his wealth was mark'd as mine—
     He had but only me.

" To win me from his tender arms,
     Unnumber'd suitors came,
Who praised me for imputed charms,
     And felt, or feigned, a flame.

" Each hour a mercenary crowd
     With richest proffers strove ;
Amongst the rest, young Edwin bowed,
     But never talked of love.

" In humble, simplest habit clad,
     No wealth nor power had he ;
Wisdom and worth were all he had,
     But these were all to me.

" And when beside me in the dale,
     He carolled lays of love,
His breath lent fragrance to the gale,
     And music to the grove.

" The blossom opening to the day,
     The dews of heaven refined,
Could nought of purity display
     To emulate his mind.

" The dew, the blossom on the tree,
    With charms inconstant shine :
Their charms were his, but, woe to me,
    Their constancy was mine.

" For still I tried each fickle art,
    Importunate and vain ;
And, while his passion touch'd my heart,
    I triumphed in his pain :

" Till, quite dejected with my scorn,
    He left me to my pride,
And sought a solitude forlorn,
    In secret, where he died.

" But mine the sorrow, mine the fault,
    And well my life shall pay ;
I'll seek the solitude he sought,
    And stretch me where he lay.

" And there, forlorn, despairing, hid,
    I'll lay me down and die ;
'Twas so for me that Edwin did,
    And so for him will I."

" Forbid it, Heaven ! " the hermit cried,
    And clasp'd her to his breast :
The wondering fair one turn'd to chide—
    'Twas Edwin's self that prest !

" Turn, Angelina, ever dear,
  My charmer, turn to see
Thy own, thy long-lost Edwin here,
  Restored to love and thee.

" Thus let me hold thee to my heart,
  And every care resign :
And shall we never, never part,
  My life,—my all that's mine ?

" No, never from this hour to part,
  We'll live and love so true—
The sigh that rends thy constant heart
  Shall break thy Edwin's too."

O. GOLDSMITH.

Elegy on the
Death of a Mad Dog

GOOD people all, of every sort,
  Give ear unto my song ;
And if you find it wondrous short,—
  It cannot hold you long.

In Islington there was a man,
   Of whom the world might say,
That still a godly race he ran,—
   Whene'er he went to pray.

A kind and gentle heart he had,
   To comfort friends and foes ;
The naked every day he clad,—
   When he put on his clothes.

And in that town a dog was found,
   As many dogs there be,
Both mongrel, puppy, whelp, and hound,
   And curs of low degree.

This dog and man at first were friends ;
  But when a pique began,
The dog, to gain some private ends,
  Went mad, and bit the man.

Around from all the neighbouring streets
  The wondering neighbours ran,
And swore the dog had lost his wits,
  To bite so good a man.

The wound it seemed both sore and sad
  To every Christian eye ;
And while they swore the dog was mad,
  They swore the man would die.

But soon a wonder came to light,
  That showed the rogues they lied ;
The man recovered of the bite,
  The dog it was that died.

O. GOLDSMITH.

∾ The Friar
of Orders Gray ∿

IT was a friar of orders gray
  Walkt forth to tell his beades ;
And he met with a lady faire
  Clad in a pilgrime's weedes.

" Now Christ thee save, thou reverend friar,
   I pray thee tell to me,
If ever at yon holy shrine
   My true love thou didst see."

" And how should I know your true love
   From many another one ? "
" O, by his cockle hat, and staff,
   And by his sandal shoone.

" But chiefly by his face and mien,
   That were so fair to view ;
His flaxen locks that sweetly curl'd,
   And eyne of lovely blue."

" O lady, he is dead and gone !
   Lady, he's dead and gone !
And at his head a green grass turfe,
   And at his heels a stone.

" Within these holy cloysters long
   He languisht, and he dyed,
Lamenting of a ladyes love,
   And playning of her pride.

·" Here bore him barefac'd on his bier
   Six proper youths and tall,
And many a tear bedew'd his grave
   Within yon kirk-yard wall."

" And art thou dead, thou gentle youth !
    And art thou dead and gone !
And didst thou die for love of me !
    Break, cruel heart of stone ! "

" O weep not, lady, weep not soe :
    Some ghostly comfort seek :
Let not vain sorrow rive thy heart,
    Ne teares bedew thy cheek."

" O do not, do not, holy friar,
    My sorrow now reprove ;
For I have lost the sweetest youth,
    That e'er wan ladyes love.

" And nowe, alas ! for thy sad losse,
    I'll evermore weep and sigh :
For thee I only wisht to live,
    For thee I wish to dye."

" Weep no more, lady, weep no more,
    Thy sorrowe is in vaine :
For violets pluckt the sweetest showers
    Will ne'er make grow againe.

" Our joys as winged dreams doe flye,
    Why then should sorrow last ?
Since grief but aggravates thy losse,
    Grieve not for what is past."

" O say not soe, thou holy friar ;
  I pray thee, say not soe :
For since my true-love dyed for mee,
  'Tis meet my tears should flow.

" And will he never come again ?
  Will he ne'er come again ?
Ah ! no, he is dead and laid in his grave,
  For ever to remain.

" His cheek was redder than the rose ;
  The comeliest youth was he ?
But he is dead and laid in his grave :
  Alas, and woe is me ! "

" Sigh no more, lady, sigh no more,
  Men were deceivers ever :
One foot on sea and one on land,
  To one thing constant never.

" Hadst thou been fond, he had been false,
  And left thee sad and heavy ;
For young men ever were fickle found,
  Since summer trees were leafy."

" Now say not soe, thou holy friar,
  I pray thee say not soe ;
My love he had the truest heart :
  O he was ever true !

" And art thou dead, thou much-lov'd youth,
    And didst thou dye for mee ?
Then farewell home ; for ever-more
    A pilgrim I will bee.

" But first upon my true-love's grave
    My weary limbs I'll lay,
And thrice I'll kiss the green-grass turf,
    That wraps his breathless clay."

" Yet stay, fair lady : rest awhile
    Beneath this cloyster wall :
See through the hawthorn blows the cold wind,
    And drizzly rain doth fall."

" O stay me not, thou holy friar ;
    O stay me not, I pray ;
No drizzly rain that falls on me,
    Can wash my fault away."

" Yet stay, fair lady, turn again,
    And dry those pearly tears ;
For see beneath this gown of gray
    Thy owne true-love appears.

" Here forc'd by grief, and hopeless love,
    These holy weeds I sought ;
And here amid these lonely walls
    To end my days I thought.

" But haply for my year of grace
  Is not yet past away,
Might I still hope to win thy love,
  No longer would I stay."

" Now farewell grief, and welcome joy
  Once more unto my heart ;
For since I have found thee, lovely youth,
  We never more will part."

T. PERCY.

The Diverting History of John Gilpin

JOHN GILPIN was a citizen
  Of credit and renown,
A train-band captain eke was he,
  Of famous London town.

John Gilpin's spouse said to her dear,
  " Though wedded we have been
These twice ten tedious years, yet we
  No holiday have seen.

" To-morrow is our wedding-day,
  And we will then repair
Unto the ' Bell ' at Edmonton,
  All in a chaise and pair.

" My sister, and my sister's child,
  Myself, and children three,
Will fill the chaise ; so you must ride
  On horseback after me."

He soon replied, " I do admire
  Of womankind but one,
And you are she, my dearest dear,
  Therefore it shall be done.

" I am a linen-draper bold,
  As all the world doth know,
And my good friend the calender
  Will lend his horse to go."

Quoth Mrs Gilpin, " That's well said ;
  And for that wine is dear,
We will be furnished with our own,
  Which is both bright and clear."

John Gilpin kissed his loving wife ;
  O'erjoyed was he to find,
That though on pleasure she was bent,
  She had a frugal mind.

The morning came, the chaise was brought,
But yet was not allowed

To drive up to the door, lest all
Should say that she was proud.

So three doors off the chaise was stayed,
  Where they did all get in ;
Six precious souls, and all agog
  To dash through thick and thin.

Smack went the whip, round went the wheels,
  Were never folks so glad,
The stones did rattle underneath,
  As if Cheapside were mad.

John Gilpin at his horse's side
  Seized fast the flowing mane,
And up he got, in haste to ride,
  But soon came down again ;

For saddle-tree scarce reached had he,
  His journey to begin,
When, turning round his head, he saw
  Three customers come in.

So down he came ; for loss of time,
  Although it grieved him sore,
Yet loss of pence, full well he knew,
  Would trouble him much more.

'Twas long before the customers
  Were suited to their mind,
When Betty screaming came downstairs,
  " The wine is left behind ! "

"Good lack!" quoth he, " yet bring it me,
  My leathern belt likewise,
In which I bear my trusty sword
  When I do exercise."

Now Mistress Gilpin (careful soul!)
  Had two stone bottles found,
To hold the liquor that she loved,
  And keep it safe and sound.

Each bottle had a curling ear,
  Through which the belt he drew,
And hung a bottle on each side,
  To make his balance true.

Then over all, that he might be
  Equipped from top to toe,
His long red cloak, well brushed and neat,
  He manfully did throw.

Now see him mounted once again
  Upon his nimble steed,
Full slowly pacing o'er the stones,
  With caution and good heed.

But finding soon a smoother road
  Beneath his well-shod feet,
The snorting beast began to trot,
  Which galled him in his seat.

So, " Fair and softly ! " John he cried,
  But John he cried in vain ;
That trot became a gallop soon,
  In spite of curb and rein.

So stooping down, as needs he must
  Who cannot sit upright,
He grasped the mane with both his hands,
  And eke with all his might.

His horse, who never in that sort
  Had handled been before,
What thing upon his back had got
  Did wonder more and more.

Away went Gilpin, neck or nought ;
  Away went hat and wig ;
He little dreamt, when he set out,
  Of running such a rig.

The wind did blow, the cloak did fly
  Like streamer long and gay,
Till, loop and button failing both,
  At last it flew away.

Then might all people well discern
  The bottles he had slung ;
A bottle swinging at each side,
  As hath been said or sung.

The dogs did bark, the children screamed,
Up flew the windows all ;

And every soul cried out, " Well done ! "
As loud as he could bawl.

Away went Gilpin—who but he ?
  His fame soon spread around ;
" He carries weight ! he rides a race !
  'Tis for a thousand pound ! "

And still as fast as he drew near,
  'Twas wonderful to view,
How in a trice the turnpike-men
  Their gates wide open threw.

And now, as he went bowing down
  His reeking head full low,
The bottles twain behind his back
  Were shattered at a blow.

Down ran the wine into the road,
  Most piteous to be seen,
Which made the horse's flanks to smoke
  As they had basted been.

But still he seemed to carry weight,
  With leathern girdle braced ;
For all might see the bottle-necks
  Still dangling at his waist.

Thus all through merry Islington
  These gambols he did play,
Until he came unto the Wash
  Of Edmonton so gay ;

And there he threw the Wash about
  On both sides of the way,
Just like unto a trundling mop,
  Or a wild goose at play.

At Edmonton his loving wife
  From the balcony spied
Her tender husband, wondering much
  To see how he did ride.

" Stop, stop, John Gilpin !—Here's the
    house ! "
  They all at once did cry ;
" The dinner waits, and we are tired ; "
  Said Gilpin—" So am I ! "

But yet his horse was not a whit
  Inclined to tarry there !
For why ?—his owner had a house
  Full ten miles off, at Ware.

So like an arrow swift he flew,
  Shot by an archer strong ;
So did he fly—which brings me to
  The middle of my song.

Away went Gilpin, out of breath,
  And sore against his will,
Till at his friend the calender's
  His horse at last stood still.

The calender, amazed to see
　　His neighbour in such trim,
Laid down his pipe, flew to the gate,
　　And thus accosted him :

" What news ? what news ? your tidings
　　　tell ;
　　Tell me you must and shall—
Say why bareheaded you are come,
　　Or why you come at all ? "

Now Gilpin had a pleasant wit,
　　And loved a timely joke ;
And thus unto the calender
　　In merry guise he spoke :

" I came because your horse would come :
　　And, if I well forebode,
My hat and wig will soon be here,
　　They are upon the road."

The calender, right glad to find
　　His friend in merry pin,
Returned him not a single word,
　　But to the house went in ;

Whence straight he came with hat and wig,
　　A wig that flowed behind,
A hat not much the worse for wear,
　　Each comely in his kind.

He held them up, and in his turn
  Thus showed his ready wit :
" My head is twice as big as yours,
  They therefore needs must fit."

" But let me scrape the dirt away,
  That hangs upon your face ;
And stop and eat, for well you may
  Be in a hungry case."

Said John, " It is my wedding-day,
  And all the world would stare
If wife should dine at Edmonton,
  And I should dine at Ware."

So turning to his horse, he said,
  " I am in haste to dine ;
'Twas for your pleasure you came here,
  You shall go back for mine."

Ah! luckless speech, and bootless boast !
  For which he paid full dear ;
For while he spake, a braying ass
  Did sing most loud and clear ;

Whereat his horse did snort, as he
  Had heard a lion roar,
And galloped off with all his might,
  As he had done before.

Away went Gilpin, and away
  Went Gilpin's hat and wig ;
He lost them sooner than at first,
  For why ?—they were too big.

Now Mistress Gilpin, when she saw
  Her husband posting down
Into the country far away,
  She pulled out half-a-crown ;

And thus unto the youth she said
  That drove them to the " Bell,"
" This shall be yours when you bring back
  My husband safe and well."

The youth did ride, and soon did meet
  John coming back amain :
Whom in a trice he tried to stop,
  By catching at his rein.

But not performing what he meant,
  And gladly would have done,
The frighted steed he frighted more,
  And made him faster run.

Away went Gilpin, and away
  Went postboy at his heels,
The postboy's horse right glad to miss
  The lumbering of the wheels.

Six gentlemen upon the road,
   Thus seeing Gilpin fly,
With postboy scampering in the rear,
   They raised the hue and cry :

" Stop thief ! stop thief !—a highwayman ! "
   Not one of them was mute ;
And all and each that passed that way
   Did join in the pursuit.

And now the turnpike-gates again
   Flew open in short space ;
The toll-men thinking, as before,
   That Gilpin rode a race.

And so he did, and won it too,
   For he got first to town ;
Nor stopped till where he had got up,
   He did again get down.

Now let us sing, Long live the King,
   And Gilpin, long live he !
And when he next doth ride abroad,
   May I be there to see !

W. Cowper.

≈ Fair Eleanor ≈

THE bell struck one, and shook the silent tower ;
The graves give up their dead : fair Eleanor
Walked by the castle gate, and lookèd in ;
A hollow groan ran through the dreary vaults.

She shrieked aloud, and sunk upon the steps,
On the cold stone her pale cheek. Sickly smells
Of death issue as from a sepulchre,
And all is silent but the sighing vaults.

Chill death withdraws his hand, and she revives ;
Amazed she finds herself upon her feet,
And, like a ghost, through narrow passages
Walking, feeling the cold walls with her hands.

Fancy returns, and now she thinks of bones
And grinning skulls, and corruptible death

Wrapt in his shroud ; and now fancies she
  hears
Deep sighs, and sees pale sickly ghosts gliding.

At length, no fancy but reality
Distracts her.   A rushing sound, and the feet
Of one that fled, approaches.—Ellen stood,
Like a dumb statue, froze to stone with fear.

The wretch approaches, crying, " The deed is
     done !
Take this, and send it by whom thou wilt send ;
It is my life—send it to Eleanor— :
He's dead, and howling after me for blood !

" Take this," he cried : and thrust into her arms
A wet napkin, wrapt about ; then rushed
Past, howling.   She received into her arms
Pale death, and followed on the wings of fear.

They passed swift through the outer gate ; the
     wretch
Howling, leaped o'er the wall into the moat,
Stifling in mud.   Fair Ellen passed the bridge,
And heard a gloomy voice cry, " Is it done ? "

As the deer wounded, Ellen flew over
The pathless plain ; as the arrows that fly
By night, destruction flies, and strikes in darkness.
She fled from fear, till at her house arrived.

Her maids await her ; on her bed she falls,
That bed of joy where erst her lord hath pressed.
" Ah woman's fear ! " she cried, " Ah cursed
     duke !
Ah my dear lord !   Ah wretched Eleanor !

" My lord was like a flower upon the brows
Of lusty May !   Ah life as frail as flower !
O ghastly Death ! withdraw thy cruel hand !
Seek'st thou that flower to deck thy horrid
    temples ?

" My lord was like a star in highest heaven
Drawn   down   to   earth   by   spells   and
    wickedness ;
My lord was like the opening eyes of day,
When western winds creep softly o'er the
    flowers.

" But he is darkened ; like the summer's noon
Clouded ; fall'n like the stately tree, cut
    down ;
The breath of heaven dwelt among his leaves,
O Eleanor, weak woman, filled with woe ! "

Thus having spoke, she raisèd up her head,
And saw the bloody napkin by her side,
Which in her arms she brought ; and now,
    tenfold
More terrified, saw it unfold itself.

Her eyes were fixed ; the bloody cloth unfolds,
Disclosing to her sight the murdered head
Of her dear lord, all ghastly pale, clotted
With gory blood ; it groaned, and thus it
    spake :

"O Eleanor, behold thy husband's head,
Who sleeping on the stones of yonder tower,
Was reft of life by the accursed duke:
A hired villain turned my sleep to death.

"O Eleanor, beware the cursed duke;
O give him not thy hand, now I am dead.
He seeks thy love; who, coward, in the night,
Hired a villain to bereave my life."

She sat with dead cold limbs, stiffened to stone;
She took the gory head up in her arms;
She kissed the pale lips; she had no tears to
    shed;
She hugged it to her breast, and groaned her
    last.

W. Blake.

≋ The Whistle ≋

I sing of a whistle, a whistle of worth,
I sing of a whistle, the pride of the North,
Was brought to the court of our good Scottish
    king,
And long with this whistle all Scotland shall
    ring.

Old Loda, still rueing the arm of Fingal,
The god of the bottle sends down from his
    hall—
" This whistle's your challenge, in Scotland get
    o'er,
And drink them to hell, sir, or ne'er see me
    more ! "

Old poets have sung, and old chronicles tell,
What champions ventured, what champions fell ;
The son of great Loda was conqueror still,
And blew on the whistle their requiem shrill.

Till Robert, the lord of the Cairn and the Scaur,
Unmatch'd at the bottle, unconquer'd in war,
He drank his poor godship as deep as the sea,
No tide of the Baltic e'er drunker than he.

Thus Robert, victorious, the trophy has gain'd,
Which now in his house has for ages remain'd ;
Till three noble chieftains, and all of his blood,
The jovial contest again have renew'd.

Three joyous good fellows, with hearts clear of
    flaw :
Craigdarroch, so famous for wit, worth, and
    law ;
And trusty Glenriddel, so skill'd in old coins ;
And gallant Sir Robert, deep-read in old wines.

Craigdarroch began, with a tongue smooth as oil,
Desiring Glenriddel to yield up the spoil ;
Or else he would muster the heads of the clan,
And once more, in claret, try which was the man.

"By the gods of the ancients!" Glenriddel
    replies,
"Before I surrender so glorious a prize,
I'll conjure the ghost of the great Rorie More,
And bumper his horn with him twenty times
    o'er."

Sir Robert, a soldier, no speech would pretend,
But he ne'er turn'd his back on his foe—or his
    friend,
Said, Toss down the whistle, the prize of the
    field,
And, knee-deep in claret, he'd die ere he'd yield.

To the board of Glenriddel our heroes repair,
So noted for drowning of sorrow and care ;
But for wine and for welcome not more known
    to fame
Than the sense, wit, and taste of a sweet lovely
    dame.

A bard was selected to witness the fray,
And tell future ages the feats of the day ;
A bard who detested all sadness and spleen,
And wish'd that Parnassus a vineyard had been.

The dinner being over, the claret they ply,
And every new cork is a new spring of joy ;

In the bands of old friendship and kindred so
   set,
And the bands grew the tighter the more they
   were wet

Gay Pleasure ran riot as bumpers ran o'er ;
Bright Phœbus ne'er witness'd so joyous a core,
And vow'd that to leave them he was quite
    forlorn,
Till Cynthia hinted he'd see them next morn.

Six bottles apiece had well wore out the night,
When gallant Sir Robert, to finish the fight,
Turn'd o'er in one bumper a bottle of red,
And swore 'twas the way that their ancestors did.

Then worthy Glenriddel, so cautious and sage,
No longer the warfare ungodly would wage ;
A high ruling-elder to wallow in wine !
He left the foul business to folks less divine.

The gallant Sir Robert fought hard to the end ;
But who can with Fate and quart-bumpers
    contend ?
Though Fate said—A hero shall perish in light ;
So up rose bright Phœbus—and down fell the
    knight.

Next up rose our bard, like a prophet in drink :
" Craigdarroch, thou'll soar when creation shall
    sink !
But if thou wouldst flourish immortal in rhyme,
Come—one bottle more—and have at the
    sublime !

" Thy line, that have struggled for Freedom
    with Bruce,
Shall heroes and patriots ever produce :
So thine be the laurel, and mine be the bay ;
The field thou hast won, by yon bright god of
    day ! "

R. BURNS.

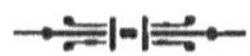

Last May

a -

Braw Wooer

LAST May a braw wooer cam down the lang glen,
    And sair wi' his love he did deave me ;
I said there was naething I hated like men,
    The deuce gae wi'm, to believe me, believe me!
    The deuce gae wi'm, to believe me !

He spak o' the darts in my bonie black e'en,
    And vow'd for my love he was dying ;
I said he might die when he likèd for Jean,
    The Lord forgie me for lying, for lying,
    The Lord forgie me for lying !

A weel-stockèd mailen—himsel for the laird—
  And marriage aff-hand, were his proffers :
I never loot on that I ken'd it, or cared,
  But thought I might hae waur offers, waur
    offers,
  But thought I might hae waur offers.

But what wad ye think? in a fortnight or less—
  The deil tak his taste to gae near her !
He up the lang loan to my black cousin Bess,
  Guess ye how, the jad! I could bear her,
    could bear her,
  Guess ye how, the jad ! I could bear her.

But a' the niest week, as I fretted wi' care,
  I gaed to the tryst o' Dalgarnock,
And wha but my fine fickle lover was there !
  I glower'd as I'd seen a warlock, a warlock,
  I glower'd as I'd seen a warlock.

But owre my left shouther I gae him a blink,
  Lest neebors might say I was saucy ;
My wooer he caper'd as he'd been in drink,
  And vow'd I was his dear lassie, dear lassie,
  And vow'd I was his dear lassie.

I spier'd for my cousin fu' couthy and sweet,
  Gin she had recover'd her hearin',
And how her new shoon fit her auld shachl't feet,
  But, heavens ! how he fell a swearin', a
    swearin',
  But, heavens ! how he fell a swearin' !

He begg'd, for gudesake, I wad be his wife,
  Or else I wad kill him wi' sorrow :
So e'en to preserve the poor body his life,
  I think I maun wed him to-morrow, to-morrow,
  I think I maun wed him to-morrow.

R. Burns.

≋ John Barleycorn ≋

There was three kings into
      the east,
    Three kings both great and
      high ;
And they hae sworn a solemn
    oath
    John Barleycorn should die.

They took a plough and
      plough'd him down,
    Put clods upon his head ;
And they hae sworn a solemn
    oath
  John Barleycorn was dead.

But the cheerfu' spring came kindly on,
    And showers began to fall ;
John Barleycorn got up again,
    And sore surprised them all.

The sultry suns of summer came,
    And he grew thick and strong,
His head weel arm'd wi' pointed spears,
    That no one should him wrong.

The sober autumn entered mild,
    When he grew wan and pale ;
His bending joints and drooping head
    Show'd he began to fail.

His colour sicken'd more and more,
    He faded into age ;
And then his enemies began
    To show their deadly rage.

They've ta'en a weapon, long and sharp,
    And cut him by the knee ;
Then tied him fast upon a cart,
    Like a rogue for forgerie.

They laid him down upon his back,
    And cudgell'd him full sore ;
They hung him up before the storm,
    And turned him o'er and o'er.

They fill'd up a darksome pit
  With water to the brim,
They heaved in John Barleycorn,
  There let him sink or swim.

They laid him out upon the floor,
  To work him further woe,
And still, as signs of life appear'd,
  They toss'd him to and fro.

They wasted, o'er a scorching flame,
  The marrow of his bones ;
But a miller used him worst of all—
  He crushed him between two stones.

And they hae ta'en his very heart's blood
  And drank it round and round ;
And still the more and more they drank,
  Their joy did more abound.

John Barleycorn was a hero bold,
  Of noble enterprise,
For if you do but taste his blood,
  'Twill make your courage rise ;

'Twill make a man forget his woe ;
  'Twill heighten all his joy :
'Twill make the widow's heart to sing,
  Though the tear were in her eye.

Then let us toast John Barleycorn,
  Each man a glass in hand ;
And may. his great posterity
  Ne'er fail in old Scotland !

R. Burns.

Lady Mary Ann

O, Lady Mary Ann
  Looks o'er the castle wa',
She saw three bonie boys
  Playing at the ba' ;
The youngest he was
  The flower amang them a' ;
My bonie laddie's young,
  But he's growin' yet.

O father ! O father !
  An' ye think it fit,
We'll send him a year
  To the college yet :
We'll sew a green ribbon
  Round about his hat,
And that will let them ken
  He's to marry yet.

Lady Mary Ann
  Was a flower i' the dew,
Sweet was its smell,
  And bonie was its hue !

And the langer it blossom'd
  The sweeter it grew ;
For the lily in the bud
  Will be bonier yet.

Young Charlie Cochrane
  Was the sprout of an aik ;
Bonie and bloomin'
  And straught was its make :
The sun took delight
  To shine for its sake,
And it will be the brag
  O' the forest yet.

The simmer is gane
  When the leaves they were green,
And the days are awa'
  That we hae seen ;
But far better days
  I trust will come again,
For my bonie laddie's young,
  But he's growin' yet.
R. Burns.

∾ The Laird o' Cockpen ∾

THE laird o' Cockpen, he's proud an' he's great,
His mind is ta'en up wi' things o' the State ;
He wanted a wife, his braw house to keep,
But favour wi' wooin' was fashious to seek.

Down by the dyke-side a lady did dwell,
At his table head he thought she'd look well,
M'Clish's ae daughter o' Clavers-ha' Lee,
A penniless lass wi' a lang pedigree.

His wig was weel pouther'd and as gude as new,
His waistcoat was white, his coat it was blue ;
He put on a ring, a sword, and cock'd hat,
And wha could refuse the laird wi' a' that ?

He took the grey mare, and rade cannily,
An' rapp'd at the yett o' Clavers-ha' Lee ;
" Gae tell Mistress Jean to come speedily ben,—
She's wanted to speak to the laird o' Cockpen."

Mistress Jean was makin' the elder-flower wine ;
" An' what brings the laird at sic a like time ? "
She put aff her apron, and on her silk gown,
Her mutch wi' red ribbons, and gaed awa' down.

An' when she cam' ben he bow'd fu' low,
An' what was his errand he soon let her know ;
Amazed was the laird when the lady said "Na,"
And wi' a laigh curtsie she turned awa'.

Dumfounder'd was he, nae sigh did he gie,
He mounted his mare—he rade cannily ;
An' aften he thought, as he gaed through the
    glen,
" She's daft to refuse the laird o' Cockpen."

CAROLINA, LADY NAIRNE.

(Stanzas added by Miss Ferrier.)

And now that the laird his exit had made,
Mistress Jean she reflected on what she had said;
" Oh, for ane I'll get better, its waur I'll get ten,
I was daft to refuse the laird o' Cockpen."

Next time that the laird and the lady were seen,
They were gaun arm-in-arm to the kirk on the
    green ;
Now she sits in the ha' like a weel-tappit hen,
But as yet there's nae chickens appear'd at
    Cockpen.

⋙ The Liddel Bower ⋙

" Oн, will ye walk the wood, lady ?
　Or will ye walk the lea ?
Or will ye gae to the Liddel Bower,
　An' rest a while wi' me ? "

" The deer lies in the wood, Douglas,
　The wind blaws on the lea ;
An' when I gae to Liddel Bower
　It shall not be wi' thee."

" The stag bells on my hills, Lady,
　The hart but and the hind ;
My flocks lie in the Border dale,
　My steeds outstrip the wind ;

" At ae blast o' my bugle horn,
　A thousand tend the ca' ;
Oh, gae wi' me to Liddel Bower—
　What ill can thee befa' ?

" D'ye mind when in that lonely bower
　We met at even tide,
I kissed your young an' rosy lips,
　An' wooed you for my bride ?

" I saw the blush break on your cheek,
　The tear stand in your e'e ;
Oh, could I ween, fair Lady Jane,
　That then ye lo'ed na me ? "

"But sair, sair hae I rued that day,
  An' sairer yet may rue ;
Ye thought na on my maiden love,
  Nor yet my rosy hue.

"Ye thought na' on my bridal bed,
  Nor vow nor tear o' mine ;
Ye thought upon the lands o' Nith,
  An' how they might be thine.

"Away! away! ye fause leman,
  Nae mair my bosom wring :
There is a bird within yon bower,
  Oh, gin ye heard it sing ! "

Red grew the Douglas' dusky cheek,
  He turned his eye away,
The gowden hilt fell to his hand ;
  "What can the wee bird say ? "

It hirpled on the bough an' sang,
  "Oh, wae's me, dame, for thee,
An' wae's me for the comely knight
  That sleeps aneath the tree !

"His cheek lies on the cauld, cauld clay,
  Nae belt nor brand has he ;
His blood is on a kinsman's spear ;
  Oh, wae's me, dame, for thee ! "

" My yeomen line the wood, lady,
  My steed stands at the tree ;
An' ye maun dree a dulefu' weird,
  Or mount and fly wi' me."

What gars Caerlaverock yeomen ride
  Sae fast in belt an' steel ?
What gars the Jardine mount his steed,
  And scour owre muir and dale ?

Why seek they up by Liddel ford,
  An' down by Tarras linn ?
The heiress o' the lands o' Nith,
  Is lost to a' her kin.

Oh, lang, lang may her mother greet,
  Down by the salt sea faem ;
An' lang, lang may the Maxwells look,
  Afore their bride come hame.

An' lang may every Douglas rue,
  An' ban the deed for aye :—
The deed was done at Liddel Bower
  About the break of day.

J. HOGG.

Ellen Irwin ;

or,

the Braes of Kirtle

FAIR Ellen Irwin, when she sate
Upon the braes of Kirtle,
Was lovely as a Grecian maid
Adorned with wreaths of myrtle ;
Young Adam Bruce beside her lay,
And there did they beguile the day
With love and gentle speeches,
Beneath the budding beeches.

From many knights and many squires
The Bruce had been selected ;
And Gordon, fairest of them all,
By Ellen was rejected.
Sad tidings to that noble youth !
For it may be proclaimed with truth,
If Bruce hath loved sincerely,
That Gordon loves as dearly.

But what is Gordon's beauteous face,
His shattered hopes and crosses,
To them 'mid Kirtle's pleasant braes,
Reclined on flowers and mosses ?

III.   D

Alas that ever he was born!
The Gordon, couched behind a thorn,
Sees them and their caressing ;
Beholds them blest and blessing.

Proud Gordon, maddened by the thoughts
That through his brain are travelling,—
Rushed forth, and at the heart of Bruce
He launched a deadly javelin !
Fair Ellen saw it as it came,
And, stepping forth to meet the same,
Did with her body cover
The youth, her chosen lover.

And, falling into Bruce's arms,
Thus died the beauteous Ellen,
Thus, from the heart of her true-love,
The mortal spear repelling.
And Bruce, as soon as he had slain
The Gordon, sailed away to Spain ;
And fought with rage incessant
Against the Moorish crescent.

But many days, and many months,
And many years ensuing,
This wretched knight did vainly seek
The death that he was wooing :
So coming his last help to crave,
Heart-broken, upon Ellen's grave
His body he extended,
And there his sorrow ended.

Now ye, who willingly have heard
The tale I have been telling,
May in Kirkconnel churchyard view
The grave of lovely Ellen :
By Ellen's side the Bruce is laid ;
And, for the stone upon its head
May no rude hand deface it,
And its forlorn HIC JACET !

W. WORDSWORTH.

≋ The Seven Sisters ; or, the
Solitude of Binnorie ≋

SEVEN daughters had Lord Archibald
All children of one mother :
I could not say in one short day
What love they bore each other.

A garland of seven lilies wrought !
Seven sisters that together dwell ;
But he, bold knight as ever fought,
Their father, took of them no thought,
He loved the wars so well.
Sing, mournfully, oh ! mournfully,
The solitude of Binnorie !

Fresh blows the wind, a western wind,
And from the shores of Erin,
Across the wave, a rover brave
To Binnorie is steering :
Right onward to the Scottish strand
The gallant ship is borne ;
The warriors leap, upon the land,
And hark ! the leader of the band
Hath blown his bugle horn.
Sing, mournfully, oh ! mournfully,
The solitude of Binnorie !

Beside a grotto of their own,
With boughs above them closing,
The seven are laid, and in the shade
They lie like fawns reposing.
But now, upstarting with affright
At noise of man and steed,
Away they fly to left, to right—
Of your fair household, father knight,
Methinks you take small heed !
Sing, mournfully, oh ! mournfully,
The solitude of Binnorie !

Away the seven fair Campbells fly,
And, over hill and hollow,
With menace proud, and insult loud,
The youthful rovers follow.
Cried they, " Your father loves to roam :
Enough for him to find
The empty house when he comes home ;
For us your yellow ringlets comb,
For us be fair and kind ! "
Sing, mournfully, oh ! mournfully,
The solitude of Binnorie !

Some close behind, some side by side,
Like clouds in stormy weather,
They run, and cry, " Nay, let us die,
And let us die together."
A lake was néar ; the shore was steep ;
There never foot had been ;
They ran, and with a desperate leap
Together plunged into the deep,
Nor ever more were seen.
Sing, mournfully, oh ! mournfully,
The solitude of Binnorie!

The stream that flows out of the lake,
As through the glen it rambles,
Repeats a moan o'er moss and stone,
For those seven lovely Campbells.
Seven little islands, green and bare,
Have risen from out the deep :

The fishers say, those sisters fair
By fairies are all buried there,
And there together sleep.
Sing, mournfully, oh ! mournfully,
The solitude of Binnorie !

W. Wordsworth.

≈ The Force of Prayer ≈

or, The Founding of Bolton's Priory.

(*A Tradition.*)

" What is good for a bootless bene ? "
With these dark words begins my tale ;
And their meaning is, Whence can comfort spring
When prayer is of no avail ?

" What is good for a bootless bene ? "
The falconer to the lady said ;
And she made answer, " Endless sorrow ! "
For she knew that her son was dead.

She knew it by the falconer's words,
And from the look of the falconer's eye ;
And from the love which was in her soul
For her youthful Romilly.

Young Romilly through Barden woods
Is ranging high and low ;
And holds a greyhound in a leash,
To let slip upon buck or doe.

The pair have reached that fearful chasm,
How tempting to bestride !
For lordly Wharf is there pent in,
With rocks on either side.

This striding-place is called The Strid,
A name which it took of yore :
A thousand years hath it borne that name,
And shall a thousand more.

And hither is young Romilly come,
And what may now forbid
That he, perhaps for the hundredth time,
Shall bound across The Strid ?

He sprang in glee,—for what cared he
That the river was strong, and the rocks were
    steep ?
But the greyhound in the leash hung back,
And checked him in his leap.

The boy is in the arms of Wharf,
And strangled by a merciless force ;
For never more was young Romilly seen
Till he rose a lifeless corse.

Now there is stillness in the vale,
And long, unspeaking sorrow :
Wharf shall be to pitying hearts
A name more sad than Yarrow.

If for a lover the lady wept,
A solace she might borrow
From death, and from the passion of death ;—
Old Wharf might heal her sorrow.

She weeps not for the wedding-day
Which was to be to-morrow :
Her hope was a farther-looking hope,
And hers is a mother's sorrow.

He was a tree that stood alone,
And proudly did its branches wave ;
And the root of this delightful tree
Was in her husband's grave !

Long, long in darkness did she sit,
And her first words were, " Let there be
In Bolton, on the field of Wharf,
A stately priory ! "

The stately priory was reared ;
And Wharf, as he moved along,
To matins joined a mournful voice,
Nor failed at even-song.

And the lady prayed in heaviness
That looked not for relief!
But slowly did her succour come,
And a patience to her grief.

Oh! there is never sorrow of heart
That shall lack a timely end,
If but to God we turn, and ask
Of Him to be our Friend!

W. WORDSWORTH.

≋ Albert Græme's Song ≋

IT was an' English ladye bright,
  (The sun shines fair on Carlisle wall,)
And she would marry a Scottish knight,
  For Love will still be lord of all.

Blithely they saw the rising sun,
  When he shone fair on Carlisle wall;
But they were sad ere day was done,
  Though Love was still the lord of all.

Her sire gave brooch and jewel fine,
  Where the sun shines fair on Carlisle wall;
Her brother gave but a flask of wine,
  For ire that Love was lord of all.

For she had lands, both meadow and lea,
   Where the sun shines fair on Carlisle wall,
And he swore her death, ere he would see
   A Scottish knight the lord of all !

That wine she had not tasted well,
   (The sun shines fair on Carlisle wall,)
When dead, in her true love's arms, she fell,
   For Love was still the lord of all !

He pierced her brother to the heart,
   Where the sun shines fair on Carlisle wall :—
So perish all would true love part,
   That Love may still be lord of all !

And then he took the cross divine,
   (Where the sun shines fair on Carlisle wall,)
And died for her sake in Palestine,
   So Love was still the lord of all.

Now all ye lovers, that faithful prove,
   (The sun shines fair on Carlisle wall,)
Pray for their souls who died for love,
   For Love shall still be lord of all !

W. Scott.

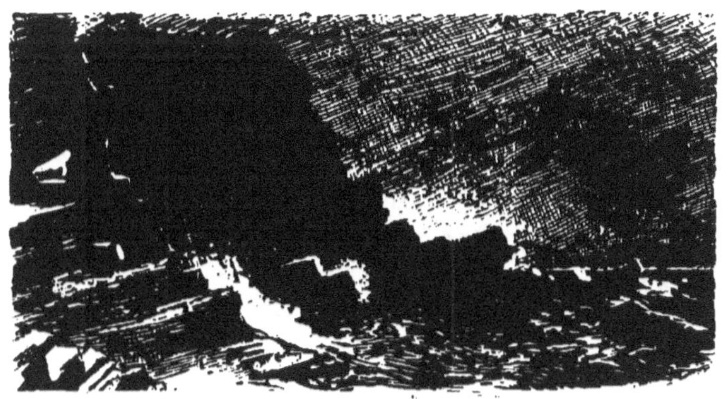

≋　Harold's Song　≋

O LISTEN, listen, ladies gay !
　No haughty feat of arms I tell ;
Soft is the note, and sad the lay,
　That mourns the lovely Rosabelle.

—" Moor, moor the barge, ye gallant crew !
　And, gentle ladye, deign to stay,
Rest thee in Castle Ravensheuch,
　Nor tempt the stormy firth to-day.

" The blackening wave is edged with white :
　To inch and rock the sea-mews fly ;
The fishers have heard the Water-Sprite,
　Whose screams forbode that wreck is nigh.

inch, isle.

"Last night the gifted Seer did view
    A wet shroud swathed round ladye gay ;
Then stay thee, Fair, in Ravensheuch :
    Why cross the gloomy firth to-day ?"—

" 'Tis not because Lord Lindesay's heir
    ·To-night at Roslin leads the ball,
But that my ladye-mother there
    Sits lonely in her castle-hall.

" 'Tis not because the ring they ride,
    And Lindesay at the ring rides well,
But that my sire the wine will chide,
    If 'tis not fill'd by Rosabelle."—

O'er Roslin all that dreary night
    A wondrous blaze was seen to gleam ;
'Twas broader than the watch-fire's light,
    And redder than the bright moon-beam.

It glared on Roslin's castled rock,
    It ruddied all the copse-wood glen,
'Twas seen from Dryden's groves of oak,
    And seen from cavern'd Hawthornden.

Seem'd all on fire that chapel proud,
    Where Roslin's chiefs uncoffin'd lie,
Each Baron for a sable shroud,
    Sheathed in his iron panoply.

Seem'd all on fire, within, around,
  Deep sacristy and altar's pale ;
Shone every pillar foliage-bound,
  And glimmer'd all the dead men's mail.

Blazed battlement and pinnet high,
  Blazed every rose-carved buttress fair—
So still they blaze, when fate is nigh
  The lordly line of high St. Clair.

There are twenty of Roslin's barons bold
  Lie buried within that proud chapelle ;
Each one the holy vault doth hold—
  But the sea holds lovely Rosabelle !

And each St. Clair was buried there,
  With candle, with book, and with knell ;
But the sea-caves rung, and the wild winds sung,
  The dirge of lovely Rosabelle.

W. Scott.

∾ Lochinvar ∾

Lady Heron's Song.

O, YOUNG Lochinvar is come out of the west,
Through all the wide Border his steed was the
    best ;
And save his good broadsword, he weapons had
    none,
He rode all unarm'd, and he rode all alone.
So faithful in love, and so dauntless in war,
There never was knight like the young Lochinvar.

He staid not for brake, and he stopp'd not for
    stone,
He swam the Eske river where ford there was
    none ;
But ere he alighted at Netherby gate,
The bride had consented, the gallant came late :
For a laggard in love, and a dastard in war,
Was to wed the fair Ellen of brave Lochinvar.

So boldly he enter'd the Netherby Hall,
Among bride's-men, and kinsmen, and brothers,
    and all :
Then spoke the bride's father, his hand on his
    sword,
(For the poor craven bridegroom said never a
    word,)
" O come ye in peace here, or come ye in war,
Or to dance at our bridal, young Lord Lochin-
    var ? "—

"I long woo'd your daughter, my suit you
    denied ;—
Love swells like the Solway, but ebbs like its
    tide ;—
And now am I come, with this lost love of mine
To lead but one measure, drink one cup of wine.
There are maidens in Scotland more lovely by far,
That would gladly be bride to the young
    Lochinvar."

The bride kiss'd the goblet : the knight took it
    up,
He quaff'd off the wine, and he threw down the
    cup.
She look'd down to blush, and she look'd up to
    sigh,
With a smile on her lips, and a tear in her eye.
He took her soft hand, ere her mother could
    bar,—
"Now tread we a measure!" said young Lochinvar.

So stately his form, and so lovely her face,
That never a hall such a galliard did grace ;
While her mother did fret, and her father did
    fume,
And the bridegroom stood dangling his bonnet
    and plume ;
And the bride-maidens whisper'd, "'Twere
    better by far,
To have match'd our fair cousin with young
    Lochinvar."

One touch to her hand, and one word in her ear,
When they reach'd the hall-door, and the
    charger stood near ;
So light to the croupe the fair lady he swung,
So light to the saddle before her he sprung !
" She is won ! we are gone, over bank, bush,
    and scaur ;
They'll have fleet steeds that follow," quoth
    young Lochinvar.

There was mounting 'mong Græmes of the
    Netherby clan ;
Forsters, Fenwicks, and Musgraves, they rode
    and they ran :
There was racing and chasing, on Cannobie
    Lee,
But the lost bride of Netherby ne'er did they
    see.
So daring in love, and so dauntless in war,
Have ye e'er heard of gallant like young Loch-
    invar ?

W. Scott.

Alice Brand

MERRY it is in the good greenwood,
   Where the mavis and merle are singing,
When the deer sweeps by, and the hounds are
     in cry,
   And the hunter's horn is ringing.

" O Alice Brand, my native land
   Is lost for love of you ;
And we must hold by wood and wold,
   As outlaws wont to do. ·

" O Alice, 'twas all for thy locks so bright,
   And 'twas all for thine eyes so blue,
That on the night of our luckless flight,
   Thy brother bold I slew.

" Now must I teach to hew the beech
   The hand that held the glaive,
For leaves to spread our lowly bed,
   And stakes to fence our cave.

III.   E

" And for vest of pall, thy fingers small,
    That wont on harp to stray,
A cloak must shear from the slaughter'd deer,
    To keep the cold away."—

" O Richard! if my brother died,
    'Twas but a fatal chance ;
For darkling was the battle tried,
    And fortune sped the lance.

" If pall and vair no more I wear,
    Nor thou the crimson sheen,
As warm, we'll say, is the russet grey,
    As gay the forest green.

" And, Richard, if our lot be hard,
    And lost thy native land,
Still Alice has her own Richard,
    And he his Alice Brand."

'Tis merry, 'tis merry, in good greenwood,
    So blithe Lady Alice is singing ;
On the beech's pride, and oak's brown side,
    Lord Richard's axe is ringing.

Up spoke the moody Elfin King,
    Who wonn'd within the hill,—
Like wind in the porch of a ruin'd church,
    His voice was ghostly shrill :

" Why sounds yon stroke on beech and oak,
  Our moonlight circle's screen ?
Or who comes here to chase the deer,
  Beloved of our Elfin Queen ?
Or who may dare on wold to wear
  The fairies' fatal green ?

" Up, Urgan, up ! to yon mortal hie,
  For thou wert christen'd man ;
For cross or sign thou wilt not fly,
  For mutter'd word or ban.

" Lay on him the curse of the wither'd heart,
  The curse of the sleepless eye ;
Till he wish and pray that his life would part,
  Nor yet find leave to die."

'Tis merry, 'tis merry, in good greenwood,
  Though the birds have still'd their singing ;
The evening blaze doth Alice raise,
  And Richard is fagots bringing.

Up Urgan starts, that hideous dwarf
  Before Lord Richard stands,
And as he cross'd and bless'd himself,
" I fear not sign," quoth the grisly elf,
  " That is made with bloody hands."

But out then spoke she, Alice Brand,
  That woman void of fear,—
" And if there's blood upon his hand,
  'Tis but the blood of deer."—

"Now loud thou liest, thou bold of mood!
    It cleaves unto his hand,
The stain of thine own kindly blood,
    The blood of Ethert Brand."

Then forward stepp'd she, Alice Brand,
    And made the holy sign,—
" And if there's blood on Richard's hand,
    A spotless hand is mine.

" And I conjure thee, Demon elf,
    By Him whom Demons fear,
To show us whence thou art thyself,
    And what thine errand here."—

" 'Tis merry, 'tis merry in Fairy-land,
    When fairy birds are singing,
When the court doth ride by their monarch's
        side,
    With bit and bridle ringing :

" And gaily shines the Fairy-land—
    But all is glistening show,
Like the idle gleam that December's beam
    Can dart on ice and snow.

" And fading, like that varied gleam,
    Is our inconstant shape,
Who now like knight and lady seem,
    And now like dwarf and ape.

"It was between the night and day,
  When the Fairy King has power,
That I sank down in a sinful fray,
And 'twixt life and death was snatched away
  To the joyless Elfin bower.

"But wist I of a woman bold,
  Who thrice my brow durst sign,
I might regain my mortal mold,
  As fair a form as thine."

She cross'd him once—she cross'd him twice—
  That lady was so brave ;
The fouler grew his goblin hue,
  The darker grew the cave.

She cross'd him thrice, that lady bold ;
  He rose beneath her hand
The fairest knight on Scottish mold,
  Her brother, Ethert Brand !

Merry it is in good greenwood,
  When the mavis and merle are singing,
But merrier were they in Dunfermline grey,
  When all the bells were ringing.

W. Scott.

≋ Jock of Hazeldean ≋

" Why weep ye by the tide, ladie ?
　Why weep ye by the tide ?
I'll wed ye to my youngest son,
　And ye sall be his bride :
And ye sall be his bride, ladie,
　Sae comely to be seen "—
But aye she loot the tears down fa'
　For Jock of Hazeldean.

" Now let this wilfu' grief be done,
　And dry that cheek so pale ;
Young Frank is chief of Errington,
　And lord of Langly-dale ;
His step is first in peaceful ha',
　His sword in battle keen "—
But aye she loot the tears down fa'
　For Jock of Hazeldean.

" A chain of gold ye sall not lack,
　Nor braid to bind your hair ;
Nor mettled hound, nor managed hawk,
　Nor palfrey fresh and fair ;
And you, the foremost o' them a',
　Shall ride our forest queen "—
But aye she loot the tears down fa'
　For Jock of Hazeldean.

The kirk was deck'd at morning-tide,
  The tapers glimmer'd fair ;
The priest and bridegroom wait the bride,
  And dame and knight are there.
They sought her baith by bower and ha' ;
  The ladie was not seen !
She's o'er the Border, and awa'
  Wi' Jock of Hazeldean.

W. Scott.

≈ Davie Gellatley's Song ≈

False love, and hast thou play'd me this
  In summer among the flowers ?
I will repay thee back again
  In winter among the showers.
Unless again, again, my love,
  Unless you turn again ;
As you with other maidens rove,
  I'll smile on other men.

  The Knight's to the mountain
    His bugle to wind ;
  The Lady's to greenwood
    Her garland to bind.
  The bower of Burd Ellen
    Has moss on the floor,
  That the step of Lord William
    Be silent and sure.

W. Scott.

∾ Elspeth's Ballad ∿

THE herring loves the merry moon-light,
   The mackerel loves the wind,
But the oyster loves the dredging sang,
   For they come of a gentle kind.

Now haud your tongue, baith wife and carle,
   And listen great and sma',
And I will sing of Glenallan's Earl
   That fought on the red Harlaw.

The cronach's cried on Bennachie,
   And doun the Don and a',
And hieland and lawland may mournfu' be
   For the sair field of Harlaw.—

They saddled a hundred milk-white steeds,
   They hae bridled a hundred black,
With a chafron of steel on each horse's head,
   And a good knight upon his back.

They hadna ridden a mile, a mile,
   A mile but barely ten,
When Donald came branking down the brae
   Wi' twenty thousand men.

Their tartans they were waving wide,
   Their glaives were glancing clear,
The pibrochs rung frae side to side,
   Would deafen ye to hear.

The great Earl in his stirrups stood,
    That Highland host to see :
"Now here a knight that's stout and good
    May prove a jeopardie :

"What would'st thou do, my squire so gay,
    That rides beside my reyne,—
Were ye Glenallan's Earl the day,
    And I were Roland Cheyne?

"To turn the rein were sin and shame,
    To fight were wond'rous peril,—
What would ye do now, Roland Cheyne,
    Were ye Glenallan's Earl?"

"Were I Glenallan's Earl this tide,
    And ye were Roland Cheyne,
The spur should be in my horse's side,
    And the bridle upon his mane.

"If they hae twenty thousand blades,
    And we twice ten times ten,
Yet they hae but their tartan plaids,
    And we are mail-clad men.

"My horse shall ride through ranks sae rude,
    As through the moorland fern,—
Then ne'er let the gentle Norman blude
    Grow cauld for Highland kerne."

W. Scott.

The Eve of St. John

THE Baron of Smaylho'me rose with day,
  He spurr'd his courser on,
Without stop or stay, down the rocky way,
  That leads to Brotherstone.

He went not with the bold Buccleuch,
  His banner broad to rear ;
He went not 'gainst the English yew,
  To lift the Scottish spear.

Yet his plate-jack was braced, and his helmet
    was laced,
  And his vaunt-brace of proof he wore :
At his saddle-gerthe was a good steel sperthe,
  Full ten pound weight and more.

The Baron returned in three days' space,
  And his looks were sad and sour ;
And weary was his courser's pace,
  As he reach'd his rocky tower.

He came not from where Ancram Moor
  Ran red with English blood ;
Where the Douglas true, and the bold Buccleuch,
  'Gainst keen Lord Evers stood.

Yet was his helmet hack'd and hew'd
  His acton pierced and tore,
His axe and his dagger with blood imbrued,—
  But it was not English gore.

He lighted at the Chapellage,
  He held him close and still ;
And he whistled thrice for his little foot-page,
  His name was English Will.

" Come thou hither, my little foot-page,
  Come hither to my knee ;
Though thou art young and tender of age,
  I think thou art true to me.

" Come, tell me all that thou hast seen,
  And look thou tell me true !
Since I from Smaylho'me tower have been,
  What did thy lady do ? "—

" My lady, each night, sought the lonely light,
  That burns on the wild Watchfold ;
For, from height to height, the beacons bright
  Of the English foemen told.

" The bittern clamour'd from the moss,
  The wind blew loud and shrill ;
Yet the craggy pathway she did cross,
  To the eiry Beacon Hill.

" I watch'd her steps, and silent came
   Where she sat her on a stone ;—
No watchman stood by the dreary flame,
   It burned all alone.

" The second night I kept her in sight,
   Till to the fire she came,
And, by Mary's might ! an Armed Knight
   Stood by the lonely flame.

" And many a word that warlike lord
   Did speak to my lady there ;
But the rain fell fast, and loud blew the blast,
   And I heard not what they were.

" The third night there the sky was fair,
   And the mountain-blast was still,
As again I watch'd the secret pair,
   On the lonesome Beacon Hill.

" And I heard her name the midnight hour,
   And name this holy eve ;
And say, ' Come this night to thy lady's bower ;
   Ask no bold Baron's leave.

" ' He lifts his spear with the bold Buccleuch ;
   His lady is all alone ;
The door she'll undo, to her knight so true,
   On the eve of good St. John.'—

" 'I cannot come ; I must not come ;
    I dare not come to thee ;
On the eve of St. John I must wander alone :
    In thy bower I may not be.'—

" ' Now, out on thee, faint-hearted knight !
    Thou shouldst not say me nay ;
For the eve is sweet, and when lovers meet,
    Is worth the whole summer's day.

" ' And I'll chain the blood-hound, and the
    warder shall not sound,
And rushes shall be strew'd on the stair ;
So, by the black rood-stone, and by holy St.
    John,
    I conjure thee, my love, to be there ! '—

" ' Though the blood-hound be mute, and the
    rush beneath my foot,
And the warder his bugle should not blow,
Yet there sleepeth a priest in a chamber to the
    east,
    And my footstep he would know.'—

" ' O fear not the priest, who sleepeth to the
    east !
For to Dryburgh the way he has ta'en ;
And there to say mass, till three days do pass,
    For the soul of a knight that is slayne.'—

" He turn'd him around and grimly he frown'd ;
   Then he laughed right scornfully—
' He who says the mass-rite for the soul of that
     knight,
   May as well say mass for me.

" ' At the lone midnight hour, when bad spirits ·
     have power,
   In thy chamber will I be.'—
With that he was gone, and my lady left alone,
   And no more did I see."

Then changed, I trow, was that bold Baron's
     brow,
   From the dark to the blood-red high ;
" Now, tell me the mien of the knight thou
     hast seen,
   For, by Mary, he shall die ! "—

" His arms shone full bright, in the beacon's
     red light :
   His plume it was scarlet and blue ;
On his shield was a hound, in a silver leash
     bound,
   And his crest was a branch of the yew."—

" Thou liest, thou liest, thou little foot-page,
   Loud dost thou lie to me !
For that knight is cold, and low laid in the mould,
   All under the Eildon-tree."—

" Yet hear but my word, my noble lord !
   For I heard her name his name ;
And that lady bright, she called the knight
   Sir Richard of Coldinghame."—

The bold Baron's brow then changed, I trow,
   From high blood-red to pale—
" The grave is deep and dark—and the corpse
     is stiff and stark—
   So I may not trust thy tale.

" Where fair Tweed flows round holy Melrose,
   And Eildon slopes to the plain,
Full three nights ago, by some secret foe,
   That gay gallant was slain.

" The varying light deceived thy sight,
   And the wild winds drown'd the name ;
For the Dryburgh bells ring, and the white
     monks do sing,
   For Sir Richard of Coldinghame ! "

He pass'd the court-gate, and he oped the
     tower-gate,
   And he mounted the narrow stair,
To the bartizan-seat, where, with maids that on
     her wait,
   He found his lady fair.

That lady sat in mournful mood
  Look'd over hill and vale ;
Over Tweed's fair flood, and Mertoun's wood,
  And all down Teviotdale.

" Now hail, now hail, thou lady bright ! "—
  " Now hail, thou Baron true !
What news, what news, from Ancram fight ?
  What news from the bold Buccleuch ? "—

" The Ancram Moor is red with gore,
  For many a Southern fell ;
And Buccleuch has charged us, evermore,
  To watch our beacons well."—

The lady blush'd red, but nothing she said :
  Nor added the Baron a word :
Then she stepp'd down the stair to her chamber
    fair,
  And so did her moody lord.

In sleep the lady mourn'd, and the Baron toss'd
    and turn'd,
  And oft to himself he said,—
" The worms around him creep, and his bloody
    grave is deep . . .
  It cannot give up the dead ! "—

It was near the ringing of matin-bell,
  The night was well-nigh done,
When a heavy sleep on that Baron fell,
  On the eve of good St. John.

The lady look'd through the chamber fair,
   By the light of a dying flame ;
And she was aware of a knight stood there—
   Sir Richard of Coldinghame !

" Alas ! away, away ! " she cried,
   " For the holy Virgin's sake ! "—
" Lady, I know who sleeps by thy side ;
   But, lady, he will not awake.

" By Eildon-tree, for long nights three,
   In bloody grave have I lain ;
The mass and the death-prayer are said for me,
   But, lady, they are said in vain.

" By the Baron's brand, near Tweed's fair strand,
   Most foully slain, I fell ;
And my restless sprite on the beacon's height,
   For a space is doom'd to dwell.

" At our trysting-place, for a certain space,
   I must wander to and fro ;
But I had not had power to come to thy bower,
   Had'st thou not conjured me so."—

Love master'd fear—her brow she cross'd ;
   " How, Richard, hast thou sped ?
And art thou saved, or art thou lost ? "—
   The vision shook his head !

III.   F

"Who spilleth life, shall forfeit life ;
　So bid thy lord believe :
That lawless love is guilt above,
　This awful sign receive."

He laid his left palm on an oaken beam ;
　His right upon her hand ;
The lady shrunk, and fainting sunk,
　For it scorch'd like a fiery brand.

The sable score, of fingers four,
　Remains on that board impress'd ;
And for evermore that lady wore
　A covering on her wrist.

There is a nun in Dryburgh bower,
　Ne'er looks upon the sun ;
There is a monk in Melrose tower
　He speaketh word to none.

That nun, who ne'er beholds the day,
　That monk, who speaks to none—
That nun was Smaylho'me's Lady gay,
　That monk the bold Baron.
　　　　　　　　　　　W. Scott.

Christabel

PART I.

'Tis the middle of night by the castle clock,
And the owls have awaken'd the crowing cock :
Tu—whit !——Tu—whoo !
And hark, again ! the crowing cock,
How drowsily it crew.

Sir Leoline, the Baron rich,
Hath a toothless mastiff bitch ;
From her kennel beneath the rock
Maketh answer to the clock,

Four for the quarters, and twelve for the
    hour ;
Ever and aye, by shine and shower,
Sixteen short howls, not over loud :
Some say, she sees my lady's shroud.

Is the night chilly and dark ?
The night is chilly, but not dark.
The thin gray cloud is spread on high,
It covers but not hides the sky.

The moon is behind, and at the full ;
And yet she looks both small and dull.
The night is chill, the cloud is gray :
'Tis a month before the month of May,
And the Spring comes slowly up this way.

The lovely lady, Christabel,
Whom her father loves so well,
What makes her in the wood so late,
A furlong from the castle gate ?
She had dreams all yesternight
Of her own betrothed knight ;
And she in the midnight wood will pray
For the weal of her lover that's far away.

She stole along, she nothing spoke,
The sighs she heaved were soft and low,
And naught was green upon the oak,
But moss and rarest mistletoe :
She kneels beneath the huge oak tree,
And in silence prayeth she.

The lady sprang up suddenly,
The lovely lady, Christabel !
It moan'd as near, as near can be,
But what it is, she cannot tell.—
On the other side it seems to be
Of the huge, broad-breasted, old oak tree.

The night is chill ; the forest bare ;
Is it the wind that moaneth bleak ?
There is not wind enough in the air
To move away the ringlet curl
From the lovely lady's cheek—
There is not wind enough to twirl
The one red leaf, the last of its clan,
That dances as often as dance it can,
Hanging so light, and hanging so high,
On the topmost twig that looks up at the sky.

Hush, beating heart of Christabel !
Jesu, Maria, shield her well !
She folded her arms beneath her cloak,
And stole to the other side of the oak.
What sees she there ?

There she sees a damsel bright,
Drest in a silken robe of white,
That shadowy in the moonlight shone :
The neck that made that white robe wan,
Her stately neck, and arms were bare ;
Her blue-vein'd feet unsandal'd were ;
And wildly glitter'd here and there
The gems entangled in her hair.
I guess, 'twas frightful there to see
A lady so richly clad as she—
Beautiful exceedingly !

" Mary mother, save me now ! "
(Said Christabel), " And who art thou ? "

The lady strange made answer meet,
And her voice was faint and sweet :—
" Have pity on my sore distress,
I scarce can speak for weariness :
Stretch forth thy hand, and have no fear ! "
Said Christabel, " How camest thou here ? "
And the lady, whose voice was faint and sweet,
Did thus pursue her answer meet :—

" My sire is of a noble line,
And my name is Geraldine :
Five warriors seized me yestermorn,
Me, even me, a maid forlorn :
They choked my cries with force and fright,
And tied me on a palfrey white.
The palfrey was as fleet as wind,
And they rode furiously behind.

They spurred amain, their steeds were white ;
And once we cross'd the shade of night.
As sure as Heaven shall rescue me,
I have no thought what men they be ;
Nor do I know how long it is
(For I have lain entranced I wis)

Since one, the tallest of the five,
Took me from the palfrey's back,
A weary woman, scarce alive.
Some mutter'd words his comrades spoke :
He placed me underneath this oak ;
He swore they would return with haste ;
Whither they went I cannot tell—
I thought I heard, some minutes past,
Sounds as of a castle bell.
Stretch forth thy hand " (thus ended she,)
" And help a wretched maid to flee."

Then Christabel stretch'd forth her hand
And comforted fair Geraldine :
" O well, bright dame ! may you command
The service of Sir Leoline ;
And gladly our stout chivalry
Will he send forth and friends withal
To guide and guard you safe and free
Home to your noble father's hall."

She rose : and forth with steps they pass'd
That strove to be, and were not, fast.
Her gracious stars the lady blest,
And thus spake on sweet Christabel :
" All our household are at rest,
The hall is silent as the cell,
Sir Leoline is weak in health
And may not well awaken'd be,
But we will move as if in stealth ;

And I beseech your courtesy
This night, to share your couch with me."

They crossed the moat, and Christabel
Took the key that fitted well ;
A little door she open'd straight,
All in the middle of the gate :
The gate that was iron'd within and without,
Where an army in battle-array had march'd out.
The lady sank, belike through pain,
And Christabel with might and main
Lifted her up, a weary weight,
Over the threshold of the gate :
Then the lady rose again,
And moved, as she were not in pain.

So, free from danger, free from fear,
They cross'd the court ; right glad they were.
And Christabel devoutly cried
To the Lady by her side,
"Praise we the Virgin all divine
Who hath rescued thee from thy distress !"
"Alas, alas !" said Geraldine,
"I cannot speak for weariness."
So, free from danger, free from fear,
They cross'd the court: right glad they were.

Outside her kennel, the mastiff old
Lay fast asleep, in moonshine cold.

The mastiff old did not awake,
Yet she an angry moan did make!
And what can ail the mastiff bitch?
Never till now she uttered yell
Beneath the eye of Christabel.
Perhaps it is the owlet's scritch :
For what can ail the mastiff bitch?

They pass'd the hall, that echoes still,
Pass as lightly as you will!
The brands were flat, the brands were dying,
Amid their own white ashes lying ;
But when the lady pass'd, there came
A tongue of light, a fit of flame ;
And Christabel saw the lady's eye,
And nothing else saw she thereby,
Save the boss of the shield of Sir Leoline tall,
Which hung in a murky old niche in the wall,
" O softly tread," said Christabel,
" My father seldom sleepeth well."

Sweet Christabel her feet doth bare,
And, jealous of the listening air,
They steal their way from stair to stair,
Now in glimmer, and now in gloom,
And now they pass the Baron's room,
As still as death, with stifled breath !
And now have reach'd her chamber door ;
And now doth Geraldine press down
The rushes of the chamber floor.

The moon shines dim in the open air,
And not a moonbeam enters here.
But they without its light can see
The chamber carved so curiously,
Carved with figures strange and sweet,
All made out of the carver's brain,
For a lady's chamber meet :

The lamp with twofold silver chain
Is fasten'd to an angel's feet.
The silver lamp burns dead and dim ;
But Christabel the lamp` will trim.
She trimm'd the lamp, and made it bright,
And left it swinging to and fro,
While Geraldine, in wretched plight,
Sank down upon the floor below.

" O weary lady, Geraldine,
I pray you, drink this cordial wine !
It is a wine of virtuous powers ;
My mother made it of wild flowers."

" And will your mother pity me,
Who am a maiden most forlorn ? "
Christabel answer'd—" Woe is me !
She died the hour that I was born.
I have heard the grey-hair'd friar tell,
How on her death-bed she did say,

That she should hear the castle-bell
Strike twelve upon my wedding-day.
O mother dear ! that thou wert here !"
" I would," said Geraldine, " she were ! "

But soon with alter'd voice, said she —
" Off, wandering mother ! Peak and pine !
I have power to bid thee flee."
Alas ! what ails poor Geraldine ?
Why stares she with unsettled eye ?
Can she the bodiless dead espy ?
And why with hollow voice cries she,
" Off, woman, off ! this hour is mine —
Though thou her guardian spirit be,
Off, woman, off ! 'tis given to me."

Then Christabel knelt by the lady's side,
And raised to heaven her eyes so blue —
" Alas ! " said she, " this ghastly ride —
Dear lady ! it hath wilder'd you ! "
The lady wiped her moist cold brow,
And faintly said, " 'Tis over now ! "

Again the wild-flower wine she drank :
Her fair large eyes 'gan glitter bright,
And from the floor whereon she sank,
The lofty lady stood upright :
She was most beautiful to see,
Like a lady of a far countrée.

And thus the lofty lady spake—
" All they, who live in the upper sky,
Do love you, holy Christabel !
And you love them, and for their sake
And for the good which me befell,
Even I, in my degree will try,
Fair maiden, to requite you well.
But now unrobe yourself ; for I
Must pray, ere yet in bed I lie."

Quoth Christabel, " So let it
    be ! "
And as the lady bade, did she.
Her gentle limbs did she undress,
And lay down in her loveliness.
But through her brain of weal and
    woe
So many thoughts moved to and
    fro,
That vain it were her lids to close ;
So half-way from the bed she rose,
And on her elbow did recline
To look at the lady Geraldine.

Beneath the lamp the lady bow'd,
And slowly rolled her eyes around ;
Then drawing in her breath aloud,
Like one that shudder'd, she unbound
The cincture from beneath her breast :
Her silken robe, and inner vest,

Dropt to her feet, and full in view,
Behold ! her bosom and half her side—
A sight to dream of, not to tell !
O shield her ! shield sweet Christabel !

Yet Geraldine nor speaks nor stirs :
Ah ! what a stricken look was hers !
Deep from within she seems half-way
To lift some weight with sick assay,
And eyes the maid and seeks delay ;
Then suddenly, as one defied,
Collects herself in scorn and pride,
And lay down by the maiden's side ! —
And in her arms the maid she took,
      Ah well-a-day !
And with low voice and doleful look
These words did say :
" In the touch of this bosom there worketh a spell,
Which is lord of thy utterance, Christabel !
Thou knowest to-night, and wilt know to-morrow,
This mark of my shame, this seal of my sorrow ;
      But vainly thou warrest,
        For this is alone in
      Thy power to declare,
        That in the dim forest
      Thou heard'st a low moaning,
And found'st a bright lady, surpassingly fair :
And didst bring her home with thee, in love and
    in charity,
To shield her and shelter her from the damp air."

THE CONCLUSION TO PART I.

It was a lovely sight to see
The Lady Christabel, when she
Was praying at the old oak tree.
  Amid the jagged shadows
  Of mossy leafless boughs
  Kneeling in the moonlight,
  To make her gentle vows;
Her slender palms together prest,
Heaving sometimes on her breast;
Her face resign'd to bliss or bale—
Her face, oh call it fair not pale,
And both blue eyes more bright
  than clear,
Each about to have a tear.

With open eyes (ah woe is me !)
Asleep, and dreaming fearfully,
Fearfully dreaming, yet, I wis,
Dreaming that alone, which is—
O sorrow and shame !   Can this be she,
The lady who knelt at the old oak tree ?
And lo ! the worker of these harms,
That holds the maiden in her arms,
Seems to slumber still and mild,
As a mother with her child.

A star hath set, a star hath risen,
O Geraldine ! since arms of thine

Have been the lovely lady's prison.
O Geraldine! one hour was thine—
Thou'st had thy will!   By tairn and rill,
The night-birds all that hour were still.
But now they are jubilant anew,
From cliff and tower, tu—whoo! tu—whoo!
Tu—whoo! tu—whoo! from wood and fell!

And, see! the lady Christabel
Gathers herself from out her trance ;
Her limbs relax, her countenance
Grows sad and soft ; the smooth thin lids
Close o'er her eyes ; and tears she sheds—
Large tears that leave the lashes bright !
And oft the while she seems to smile
As infants at a sudden light !

Yea, she doth smile, and she doth weep,
Like a youthful hermitess,
Beauteous in a wilderness,
Who, praying always, prays in sleep.
And, if she move unquietly,
Perchance, 'tis but the blood so free,
Comes back and tingles in her feet.
No doubt, she hath a vision sweet.
What if her guardian spirit 'twere ?
What if she knew her mother near ?
But this she knows, in joys and woes,
That saints will aid if men will call :
For the blue sky bends over all !

PART II.

" Each matin bell," the Baron saith,
" Knells us back to a world of death."
These words Sir Leoline first said,
When he rose and found his lady dead :
These words Sir Leoline will say,
Many a morn to his dying day!

And hence the custom and law began,
That still at dawn the sacristan,
Who duly pulls the heavy bell,
Five and forty beads must tell
Between each stroke—a warning knell,
Which not a soul can choose but hear
From Bratha Head to Windermere.

Saith Bracy the bard, " So let it knell !
And let the drowsy sacristan
Still count as slowly as he can !
There is no lack of such, I ween,
As well fill up the space between."
In Langdale Pike and Witch's Lair,
And Dungeon-ghyll so foully rent,
With ropes of rock and bells of air
Three sinful sextons' ghosts are pent,
Who all give back, one after t'other,
The death-note to their living brother ;

III.   G

And oft too, by the knell offended,
Just as their one ! two ! three ! is ended,
The devil mocks the doleful tale
With a merry peal from Borrowdale.

The air is still ! through mist and cloud
That merry peal comes ringing loud ;
And Geraldine shakes off her dread;
And rises lightly from the bed ;
Puts on her silken vestments white,
And tricks her hair in lovely plight,
And nothing doubting of her spell
Awakens the lady Christabel.
" Sleep you, sweet lady Christabel ?
I trust that you have rested well."

And Christabel awoke and spied
The same who lay down by her side—
Oh rather say, the same whom she
Raised up beneath the old oak tree !
Nay, fairer yet ! and yet more fair !
For she belike hath drunken deep
Of all the blessedness of sleep !
And while she spake, her looks, her air,
Such gentle thankfulness declare,
That (so it seem'd) her girded vests
Grew tight beneath her heaving breasts.
" Sure I have sinn'd !" said Christabel,
" Now heaven be praised if all be well !"

And in low faltering tones, yet sweet,
Did she the lofty lady greet,
With such perplexity of mind
As dreams too lively leave behind.

So quickly she rose, and quickly array'd
Her maiden limbs, and having pray'd
That He, who on the Cross did groan,
Might wash away her sins unknown,
She forthwith led fair Geraldine
To meet her sire, Sir Leoline.

The lovely maid and the lady tall
Are pacing both into the hall,
And pacing on through page and groom
Enter the Baron's presence-room.

The Baron rose, and while he prest
His gentle daughter to his breast,
With cheerful wonder in his eyes
The lady Geraldine he espies,
And gave such welcome to the same,
As might beseem so bright a dame!

But when he heard the lady's tale,
And when she told her father's name,
Why wax'd Sir Leoline so pale,
Murmuring o'er the name again,
Lord Roland de Vaux of Tryermaine?

Alas! they had been friends in youth;
But whispering tongues can poison truth;
And constancy lives in realms above;
And life is thorny; and youth is vain;
And to be wroth with one we love,
Doth work like madness in the brain.
And thus it chanced, as I divine,
With Roland and Sir Leoline.
Each spake words of high disdain
And insult to his heart's best brother:
They parted—ne'er to meet again!
But never either found another
To free the hollow heart from paining—
They stood aloof, the scars remaining,
Like cliffs which had been rent asunder;
A dreary sea now flows between.
But neither heat, nor frost, nor thunder,
Shall wholly do away, I ween,
The marks of that which once hath been.
Sir Leoline, a moment's space,
Stood gazing on the damsel's face:
And the youthful Lord of Tryermaine
Came back upon his heart again.

Oh then the Baron forgot his age,
His noble heart swelled high with rage;
He swore by the wounds in Jesu's side,
He would proclaim it far and wide
With trump and solemn heraldry,
That they who thus had wrong'd the dame

'Were base as spotted infamy !
" And if they dare deny the same,
My herald shall appoint a week,
And let the recreant traitors seek
My tourney court—that there and then
I may dislodge their reptile souls
From the bodies and forms of men ! "
He spake : his eye in lightning rolls !
For the lady was ruthlessly seized ; and he
    kenned
In the beautiful lady the child of his friend.

And now the tears were on his face,
And fondly in his arms' he took
Fair Geraldine, who met the embrace,
Prolonging it with joyous look.
Which when she viewed, a vision fell
Upon the soul of Christabel,
The vision of fear, the touch and pain !
She shrunk and shudder'd, and saw again—
(Ah ! woe is me ! Was it for thee,
Thou gentle maid ! such sights to see ?)

Again she saw that bosom old,
Again she felt that bosom cold,
And drew in her breath with a hissing sound :
Whereat the Knight turn'd wildly round,
And nothing saw but his own sweet maid,
With eyes upraised, as one that pray'd.

The touch, the sight, had pass'd away,
And in its stead that vision blest,
Which comforted her after-rest,
While in the lady's arms she lay,
Had put a rapture in her breast,
And on her lips and o'er her eyes
Spread smiles like light !
                    With new surprise,
" What ails then my beloved child ? "
The Baron said—His daughter mild
Made answer, " All will yet be well ! "
I ween she had no power to tell
Aught else : so mighty was the spell.
Yet he, who saw this Geraldine,
Had deemed her sure a thing divine,
Such sorrow with such grace she blended,
As if she feared she had offended
Sweet Christabel, that gentle maid !
And with such lowly tones she pray'd,
She might be sent without delay
Home to her father's mansion.

                    " Nay !
Nay, by my soul ! " said Leoline.
" Ho ! Bracy the bard, the charge be thine !
Go thou, with music sweet and loud,
And take two steeds with trappings proud,
And take the youth whom thou lov'st best
To bear thy harp and learn thy song,
And clothe you both in solemn vest,

And over the mountains haste along,
Lest wandering folk that are abroad
Detain you on the valley road.
And when he has cross'd the Irthing flood,
My merry bard! he hastes, he hastes
Up Knorren moor, through Halegarth Wood,
And reaches soon that castle good
Which stands and threatens Scotland's wastes.

" Bard Bracy! bard Bracy! your horses are fleet,
Ye must ride up the hall, your music so sweet,
More loud than your horses' echoing feet!
And loud and loud to Lord Roland call
' Thy daughter is safe in Langdale Hall!
Thy beautiful daughter is safe and free—
Sir Leoline greets thee thus through me.
He bids thee come without delay
With all thy numerous array,
And take thy lovely daughter home :
And he will meet thee on the way
With all his numerous array
White with their panting palfreys' foam :
And, by mine honour! I will say
That I repent me of the day
When I spake words of fierce disdain
To Roland de Vaux of Tryermaine!
For since that evil hour hath flown,
Many a summer sun hath shone ;
Yet ne'er found I a friend again
Like Roland de Vaux of Tryermaine."

The lady fell, and clasp'd his knees,
Her face upraised, her eyes o'erflowing ;
And Bracy replied with faltering voice,
His gracious hail on all bestowing ;—
" Thy words, thou sire of Christabel,
Are sweeter than my harp can tell ;
Yet might I gain a boon of thee,
This day my journey should not be ;
So strange a dream hath come to me ;
That I had vow'd with music loud
To clear yon wood from thing unblest,
Warn'd by a vision in my rest !
For in my sleep I saw that dove,
That gentle bird, whom thou dost love,
And call'st by thy own daughter's name—
Sir Leoline ! I saw the same,
Fluttering, and uttering fearful moan,
Among the green herbs in the forest alone.
Which when I saw and when I heard,
I wonder'd what might ail the bird ;
For nothing near it could I see,
Save the grass and green herbs underneath
    the old tree.

" And in my dream methought I went
To search out what might there be found ;
And what the sweet bird's trouble meant,
That thus lay fluttering on the ground.
I went and peer'd, and could descry
No cause for her distressful cry ;

But yet for her dear lady's sake
I stoop'd, methought, the dove to take,
When lo ! I saw a bright green snake
Coil'd around its wings and neck.
Green as the herbs on which it couch'd,
Close by the dove's its head it crouch'd ;
And with the dove it heaves and stirs,
Swelling its neck as she swell'd hers !
I woke ; it was the midnight hour,
The clock was echoing in the tower ;
But though my slumber was gone by,
This dream it would not pass away—
It seems to live upon my eye !
And thence I vow'd this self-same day,
With music strong and saintly song,
To wander through the forest bare,
Lest aught unholy loiter there."

Thus Bracy said : the Baron, the while
Half-listening, heard him with a smile ;
Then turned to Lady Geraldine,
His eyes made up of wonder and love ;
And said in courtly accents fine,
" Sweet maid, Lord Roland's beauteous dove,
With arms more strong than harp or song,
Thy sire and I will crush the snake ! "
He kiss'd her forehead as he spake,
And Geraldine, in maiden wise,
Casting down her large bright eyes,

With blushing cheek and courtesy fine,
She turn'd her from Sir Leoline ;
Softly gathering up her train,
That o'er her right arm fell again ;
And folded her arms across her chest,
And crouched her head upon her breast,
And look'd askance at Christabel——
Jesu, Maria, shield her well !

A snake's small eye blinks dull and shy,
And the lady's eyes they shrunk in her head,
Each shrunk up to a serpent's eye,
And with somewhat of malice, and more
    of dread
At Christabel she look'd askance !—
One moment—and the sight was fled !
But Christabel in dizzy trance
Stumbling on the unsteady ground
Shudder'd aloud, with a hissing sound ;
And Geraldine again turn'd round,
And like a thing, that sought relief,
Full of wonder and full of grief,
She roll'd her large bright eyes divine
Wildly on Sir Leoline.

The maid, alas ! her thoughts are gone,
She nothing sees—no sight but one !
The maid, devoid of guile and sin,
I know not how, in fearful wise

So deeply had she drunken in
That look, those shrunken serpent eyes,
That all her features were resign'd
To this sole image in her mind :
And passively did imitate
That look of dull and treacherous hate.
And thus she stood, in dizzy trance,
Still picturing that look askance,
With forced unconscious sympathy,
Full before her father's view——
As far as such a look could be,
In eyes so innocent and blue !
And when the trance was o'er, the maid
Paused awhile, and inly pray'd :
Then falling at the Baron's feet,
" By my mother's soul do I entreat
That thou this woman send away ! "
She said : and more she could not say :
For what she knew she could not tell,
O'er-master'd by the mighty spell.

Why is thy cheek so wan and wild,
Sir Leoline ?   Thy only child
Lies at thy feet, thy joy, thy pride,
So fair, so innocent, so mild ;
The same, for whom thy lady died !
Oh by the pangs of her dear mother
Think thou no evil of thy child !
For her, and thee, and for no other,

She pray'd the moment ere she died,
Pray'd that the babe for whom she died,
Might prove her dear lord's joy and pride !
   That prayer her deadly pangs beguiled,
     Sir Leoline !
And wouldst thou wrong thy only child,
     Her child and thine ?

Within the Baron's heart and brain
If thoughts like these had any share,
They only swell'd his rage and pain,
And did but work confusion there.
His heart was cleft with pain and rage,
His cheeks they quiver'd, his eyes were wild,
Dishonour'd thus in his old age,
Dishonour'd by his only child,
And all his hospitality
To the wrong'd daughter of his friend
By more than woman's jealousy
Brought thus to a disgraceful end—
He roll'd his eye with stern regard
Upon the gentle minstrel bard,
And said in tones abrupt, austere—
" Why, Bracy ! dost thou loiter here ?
I bade thee hence ! " The bard obey'd ;
And turning from his own sweet maid,
The aged knight, Sir Leoline,
Led forth the Lady Geraldine !

THE CONCLUSION TO PART II.

A LITTLE child, a limber elf,
Singing, dancing to itself,
A fairy thing with red round cheeks
That always finds, and never seeks,
Makes such a vision to the sight
As fills a father's eyes with light ;
And pleasures flow in so thick and fast
Upon his heart, that he at last
Must needs express his love's excess
With words of unmeant bitterness.
Perhaps 'tis pretty to force together
Thoughts so all unlike each other ;
To mutter and mock a broken charm,
To dally with wrong that does no harm.
Perhaps 'tis tender too and pretty
At each wild word to feel within
A sweet recoil of love and pity.
And what, if in a world of sin
(Oh sorrow and shame should this be true !)
Such giddiness of heart and brain
Comes seldom save from rage and pain,
So talks as it's most used to do.

S. T. COLERIDGE.

The Rime of ∾
the Ancient Mariner ∾

It is an ancient Mariner,
And he stoppeth one of three.
" By thy long grey beard and glittering eye,
Now wherefore stopp'st thou me ?

" The Bridegroom's doors are open'd wide,
And I am next of kin ;
The guests are met, the feast is set :—
May'st hear the merry din."

He holds him with his skinny hand,
" There was a ship," quoth he.
" Hold off ! unhand me, grey-beard loon ! "
Eftsoons his hand dropt he.

He holds him with his glittering eye—
The wedding-guest stood still,
And listens like a three-years' child :
The Mariner hath his will.

The wedding-guest sat on a stone ;
He cannot choose but hear ;
And thus spake on that ancient man,
The bright-eyed Mariner :—

" The ship was cheer'd, the harbour clear'd,
Merrily did we drop
Below the kirk, below the hill,
Below the lighthouse top.

" The sun came up upon the left,
Out of the sea came he !
And he shone bright, and on the right
Went down into the sea.

" Higher and higher every day,
Till over the mast at noon—"
The wedding-guest here beat his breast,
For he heard the loud bassoon.

The bride hath paced into the hall,
Red as a rose is she ;
Nodding their heads before her goes
The merry minstrelsy.

The wedding-guest he beat his breast,
Yet he cannot choose but hear ;
And thus spake on that ancient man,
The bright-eyed Mariner.

" And now the storm-blast came, and he
Was tyrannous and strong :
He struck with his o'ertaking wings,
And chased us south along.

" With sloping masts and dipping prow,
As who pursued with yell and blow
Still treads the shadow of his foe
And forward bends his head,
The ship drove fast, loud roar'd the blast,
And southward aye we fled.

" And now there came both mist and snow,
And it grew wondrous cold ;
And ice, mast-high, came floating by,
As green as emerald.

" And through the drifts the snowy clifts
Did send a dismal sheen :
Nor shapes of men nor beasts we ken—
The ice was all between.

" The ice was here, the ice was there,
The ice was all around :
It crack'd and growl'd, and roar'd and howl'd,
Like noises in a swound !

" At length did cross an Albatross :
Thorough the fog it came :
As if it had been a Christian soul,
We hail'd it in God's name.

" It ate the food it ne'er had eat,
And round and round it flew.
The ice did split with a thunder-fit ;
The helmsman steer'd us through !

" And a good south wind sprung up behind ;
The Albatross did follow,
And every day, for food or play,
Came to the mariner's hollo !

" In mist or cloud, on mast or shroud,
It perch'd for vespers nine ;
Whiles all the night, through fog-smoke
     white,
Glimmer'd the white moon-shine."

III.   H

" God save thee, ancient Mariner !
From the fiends, that plague thee thus !—
Why look'st thou so ? "—" With my cross-
  bow
I shot the Albatross ! "

PART II.

" THE sun now rose upon the right :
Out of the sea came he,
Still hid in mist, and on the left
Went down into the sea.

" And the good south wind still blew
  behind,
But no sweet bird did follow,
Nor any day, for food or play,
Came to the mariner's hollo !

" And I had done a hellish thing,
And it would work 'em woe ;
For all averred I had kill'd the bird
That made the breeze to blow.
' Ah, wretch ! ' said they, ' the bird to slay,
That made the breeze to blow ! '

" Nor dim nor red, like God's own head,
The glorious sun uprist :
Then all averred I had kill'd the bird
That brought the fog and mist.
' 'Twas right,' said they, ' such birds to slay,
That bring the fog and mist.'

" The fair breeze blew, the white foam flew,
The furrow follow'd free :
We were the first that ever burst
Into that silent sea.

" Down dropt the breeze, the sails dropt
　　down,
'Twas sad as sad could be ;
And we did speak only to break
The silence of the sea !

" All in a hot and copper sky,
The bloody sun, at noon,
Right up above the mast did stand,
No bigger than the moon.

" Day after day, day after day,
We stuck, nor breath nor motion ;
As idle as a painted ship
Upon a painted ocean.

" Water, water, everywhere,
And all the boards did shrink ;
Water, water, everywhere,
Nor any drop to drink.

" The very deep did rot : O Christ !
That ever this should be !
Yea, slimy things did crawl with legs
Upon the slimy sea.

" About, about, in reel and rout,
The death-fires danced at night ;
The water, like a witch's oils,
Burnt green, and blue and white.

" And some in dreams assured were
Of the spirit that plagued us so :
Nine fathom deep he had follow'd us
From the land of mist and snow.

" And every tongue, through utter drought,
Was withered at the root ;
We could not speak, no more than if
We had been choked with soot.

" Ah ! well a-day ! what evil looks
Had I from old and young !
Instead of the cross, the Albatross
About my neck was hung."

PART III.

" There pass'd a weary time. Each throat
Was parch'd, and glazed each eye.
A weary time ! a weary time !
How glazed each weary eye !
When looking westward I beheld
A something in the sky.

" At first it seem'd a little speck,
And then it seem'd a mist :
It moved and moved, and took at last
A certain shape, I wist.

" A speck, a mist, a shape, I wist !
And still it near'd and near'd :
As if it dodged a water-sprite,
It plunged and tack'd and veer'd.

" With throats unslaked, with black lips
    baked,
We could not laugh nor wail ;
Through utter drought all dumb we stood !
I bit my arm, I suck'd the blood,
And cried, ' A sail ! a sail ! '

" With throats unslaked, with black lips
    baked,
Agape they heard me call :
Gramercy ! they for joy did grin,
And all at once their breath drew in,
As they were drinking all.

" ' See ! see ! ' (I cried) ' she tacks no more !
Hither to work us weal,
Without a breeze, without a tide,
She steadies with upright keel ! '

" The western wave was all a-flame.
The day was well-nigh done !
Almost upon the western wave
Rested the broad bright sun ;
When that strange shape drove suddenly
Betwixt us and the sun.

" And straight the sun was fleck'd with bars,
(Heaven's Mother send us grace !)
As if through a dungeon-grate he peer'd,
With broad and burning face.

" ' Alas ! ' (thought I, and my heart beat
    loud)
' How fast she nears and nears !
Are those her sails that glance in the sun,
Like restless gossameres ?

" ' Are those her ribs through which the sun
Did peer, as through a grate ?
And is that Woman all her crew ?
Is that a Death ? and are there two ?
Is Death that woman's mate ? '

" Her lips were red, her looks were free,
Her locks were yellow as gold :
Her skin was as white as leprosy,
The night-mare Life-in-Death was she,
Who thicks man's blood with cold.

" The naked hulk alongside came,
And the twain were casting dice ;
' The game is done ! I've won, I've won ! '
Quoth she, and whistles thrice.

" The sun's rim dips ; the stars rush out :
At one stride comes the dark ;
With far-heard whisper, o'er the sea,
Off shot the spectre-bark.

" We listen'd and look'd sideways up !
Fear at my heart, as at a cup,
My life-blood seem'd to sip !
The stars were dim, and thick the night,
The steersman's face by his lamp gleam'd
        white !
From the sails the dew did drip—
Till clomb above the eastern bar
The horned moon, with one bright star
Within the nether tip.

" One after one, by the star-dogged moon,
Too quick for groan or sigh,
Each turn'd his face with a ghastly pang,
And cursed me with his eye.

" Four times fifty living men
(And I heard nor sigh nor groan)
With heavy thump, a lifeless lump,
They dropp'd down one by one.

"The souls did from their bodies fly—
They fled to bliss or woe!
And every soul, it pass'd me by,
Like the whizz of my cross-bow!"

PART IV.

"I FEAR thee, ancient Mariner!
I fear thy skinny hand!
And thou art long, and lank, and brown,
As is the ribb'd sea-sand.

"I fear thee and thy glittering eye,
And thy skinny hand, so brown."—
"Fear not, fear not, thou wedding-guest!
This body dropt not down.

"Alone, alone, all, all alone,
Alone on a wide, wide sea!
And never a saint took pity on
My soul in agony.

"The many men, so beautiful!
And they all dead did lie:
And a thousand thousand slimy things
Lived on, and so did I.

"I look'd upon the rotting sea,
And drew my eyes away;
I look'd upon the rotting deck,
And there the dead men lay.

" I look'd to Heaven, and tried to pray ;
But or ever a prayer had gusht,
A wicked whisper came, and made
My heart as dry as dust.

" I closed my lids, and kept them close,
And the balls like pulses beat ;
For the sky and the sea, and the sea and
    the sky,
Lay like a load on my weary eye,
And the dead were at my feet.

" The cold sweat melted from their limbs,
 Nor rot nor reek did they :
The look with which they look'd on me
Had never pass'd away.

" An orphan's curse would drag to hell
A spirit from on high ;
But oh ! more horrible than that
Is the curse in a dead man's eye !
Seven days, seven nights, I saw that curse,
And yet I could not die.

" The moving moon went up the sky
And nowhere did abide ;
Softly she was going up,
And a star or two beside—

" Her beams bemock'd the sultry main,
Like April hoar-frost spread ;

But where the ship's huge shadow lay,
The charmed water burnt alway
A still and awful red.

" Beyond the shadow of the ship,
I watch'd the water-snakes ;
They moved in tracks of shining white,
And when they rear'd, the elfish light
Fell off in hoary flakes.

" Within the shadow of the ship
I watch'd their rich attire :
Blue, glossy green, and velvet black,
They coil'd and swam, and every track
Was a flash of golden fire.

" O happy living things ! no tongue
Their beauty might declare :
A spring of love gush'd from my heart,
And I blessed them unaware !
Sure my kind saint took pity on me,
And I blessed them unaware.

" The selfsame moment I could pray,
And from my neck so free
The Albatross fell off, and sank
Like lead into the sea."

PART V.

" O sleep ! it is a gentle thing,
Beloved from pole to pole !
To Mary Queen the praise be given !
She sent the gentle sleep from Heaven,
That slid into my soul.

" The silly buckets on the deck,
That had so long remained,
I dreamt that they were fill'd with dew ;
And when I awoke it rain'd.

" My lips were wet, my throat was cold,
My garments all were dank ;
Sure I had drunken in my dreams,
And still my body drank.

" I moved, and could not feel my limbs :
I was so light—almost
I thought that I had died in sleep,
And was a blessed ghost.

" And soon I heard a roaring wind :
It did not come anear,
But with its sound it shook the sails
That were so thin and sere.

" The upper air burst into life !
And a hundred fire-flags sheen,
To and fro they were hurried about !
And to and fro, and in and out,
The wan stars danced between.

" And the coming wind did roar more loud,
And the sails did sigh like sedge,
And the rain pour'd down from one black
    cloud ;
The moon was at its edge.

" The thick black cloud was cleft, and still
The moon was at its side :
Like waters shot from some high crag
The lightning fell with never a jag,
A river steep and wide.

" The loud wind never reach'd the ship,
Yet now the ship moved on !
Beneath the lightning and the moon
The dead men gave a groan.

" They groan'd, they stirr'd, they all uprose,
Nor spake, nor moved their eyes ;
It had been strange, even in a dream,
To have seen those dead men rise.

" The helmsman steer'd, the ship moved on ;
Yet never a breeze up-blew ;
The mariners all 'gan work the ropes
Where they were wont to do :
They raised their limbs like lifeless tools—
We were a ghastly crew.

" The body of my brother's son
Stood by me, knee to knee :
The body and I pull'd at one rope,
But he said nought to me."

" I fear thee, ancient Mariner ! "
" Be calm, thou Wedding-Guest !
'Twas not those souls that fled in pain,
Which to their corses came again,
But a troop of spirits blest :

" For when it dawn'd—they dropp'd their
        arms,
And clustered round the mast ;
Sweet sounds rose slowly through their
        mouths,
And from their bodies pass'd.

" Around, around, flew each sweet sound,
Then darted to the sun ;
Slowly the sounds come back again,
Now mixed, now one by one.

" Sometimes a-dropping from the sky
I heard the skylark sing ;
Sometimes all little birds that are,
How they seem'd to fill the sea and air
With their sweet jargoning !

" And now 'twas like all instruments,
Now like a lonely flute ;
And now it is an angel's song,
That makes the heavens be mute.

" It ceased ; yet still the sails made on
A pleasant noise till noon,
A noise like of a hidden brook
In the leafy month of June,
That to the sleeping woods all night
Singeth a quiet tune.

" Till noon we quietly sail'd on,
Yet never a breeze did breathe :
Slowly and smoothly went the ship,
Moved onward from beneath.

" Under the keel nine fathom deep,
From the land of mist and snow,
The spirit slid,—and it was he
That made the ship to go.
The sails at noon left off their tune,
And the ship stood still also.

"The sun, right up above the mast,
Had fix'd her to the ocean ;
But in a minute she 'gan stir,
With a short uneasy motion—
Backwards and forwards half her length
With a short uneasy motion.

"Then like a pawing horse let go,
She made a sudden bound :
It flung the blood into my head,
And I fell down in a swound.

"How long in that same fit I lay
I have not to declare ;
But ere my living life return'd,
I heard and in my soul discern'd
Two voices in the air.

"'Is it he ?' quoth one, 'Is this the man ?
By Him who died on cross,
With his cruel bow he laid full low,
The harmless albatross.

"'The spirit who bideth by himself
In the land of mist and snow,
He loved the bird that loved the man
Who shot him with his bow.'

"The other was a softer voice,
As soft as honey-dew :
Quoth he, 'The man hath penance done
And penance more will do.'"

PART VI.

First Voice.

" ' But tell me, tell me ! speak again,
Thy soft response renewing—
What makes that ship drive on so fast ?
What is the ocean doing ? '

Second Voice.

" ' Still as a slave before his lord,
The ocean hath no blast ;
His great bright eye most silently
Up to the moon is cast—

" ' If he may know which way to go,
For she guides him smooth or grim.
See, brother, see ! how graciously
She looketh down on him.'

First Voice.

" ' But why drives on that ship so fast,
Without or wave or wind ? '

Second Voice.

" ' The air is cut away before,
And closes from behind.

Fly, brother, fly! more high, more high!
Or we shall be belated :
For slow and slow that ship will go,
When the Mariner's trance is abated.'

" I woke, and we were sailing on
As in a gentle weather :
'Twas night, calm night, the moon was high ;
The dead men stood together.

" All stood together on the deck,
For a charnel-dungeon fitter :
All fix'd on me their stony eyes,
That in the moon did glitter.

"The pang, the curse, with which they died,
Had never pass'd away :
I could not draw my eyes from theirs,
Nor turn them up to pray.

" And now this spell was snapt : once more
I view'd the ocean green,
And look'd far forth, yet little saw
Of what had else been seen—

" Like one that on a lonesome road
Doth walk in fear and dread,
And having once turn'd round, walks on
And turns no more his head ;
Because he knows a frightful fiend
Doth close behind him tread.

III.   I

"But soon there breathed a wind on me,
Nor sound nor motion made :
Its path was not upon the sea,
In ripple or in shade.

"It raised my hair, it fann'd my cheek
Like a meadow-gale of spring—
It mingled strangely with my fears,
Yet it felt like a welcoming.

"Swiftly, swiftly flew the ship,
Yet she sail'd softly too :
Sweetly, sweetly blew the breeze—
On me alone it blew.

"O! dream of joy! is this indeed
The lighthouse top I see?
Is this the hill? is this the kirk?
Is this mine own countree?

"We drifted o'er the harbour-bar,
And I with sobs did pray—
'O let me be awake, my God!
Or let me sleep alway.'

"The harbour-bay was clear as glass,
So smoothly it was strewn!
And on the bay the moonlight lay,
And the shadow of the moon.

" The rock shone bright, the kirk no less,
That stands above the rock :
The moonlight steep'd in silentness
The steady weathercock.

" And the bay was white with silent light,
Till rising from the same,
Full many shapes, that shadows were,
In crimson colours came.

" A little distance from the prow
Those crimson shadows were :
I turn'd my eyes upon the deck—
Oh, Christ ! what saw I there ?

" Each corse lay flat, lifeless and flat,
And, by the holy rood !
A man all light, a seraph-man,
On every corse there stood.

" This seraph-band, each waved his hand :
It was a heavenly sight !
They stood as signals to the land,
Each one a lovely light :

" This seraph-band, each waved his hand,
No voice did they impart—
No voice ; but oh ! the silence sank
Like music on my heart.

"But soon I heard the dash of oars,
I heard the pilot's cheer;
My head was turn'd perforce away
And I saw a boat appear.

"The pilot, and the pilot's boy,
I heard them coming fast:
Dear Lord in Heaven! it was a joy
The dead men could not blast.

"I saw a third—I heard his voice:
It is the Hermit good!
He singeth aloud his godly hymns
That he makes in the wood.
He'll shrieve my soul, he'll wash away
The Albatross's blood."

PART VII.

"This Hermit good lives in that wood,
Which slopes down to the sea.
How loudly his sweet voice he rears!
He loves to talk with marineres
That come from a far countree.

"He kneels at morn, and noon, and eve—
He hath a cushion plump;
It is the moss that wholly hides
The rotted old oak-stump.

" The skiff-boat neared : I heard them talk,
' Why, this is strange, I trow !
Where are those lights so many and fair,
That signal made but now ?

" ' Strange, by my faith ! ' the Hermit said—
' And they answer'd not our cheer !
The planks look warp'd ! and see those sails
How thin they are and sere !
I never saw aught like to them,
Unless perchance it were

" ' Brown skeletons of leaves that lag
My forest-brook along ;
When the ivy-tod is heavy with snow,
And the owlet whoops to the wolf below,
That eats the she-wolf's young.'

" ' Dear Lord ! it hath a fiendish look,'—
(The pilot made reply).
' I am a-feared.'—' Push on, push on ! '
Said the Hermit cheerily.

" The boat came closer to the ship,
But I nor spake nor stirr'd ;
The boat came close beneath the ship,
And straight a sound was heard.

" Under the water it rumbled on,
Still louder and more dread :
It reach'd the ship, it split the bay ;
The ship went down like lead.

" Stunned by that loud and dreadful sound,
Which sky and ocean smote,
Like one that hath been seven days drown'd,
My body lay afloat ; .
But swift as dreams, myself I found
Within the pilot's boat.

" Upon the whirl, where sank the ship
The boat spun round and round ;
And all was still, save that the hill
Was telling of the sound.

" I moved my lips—the pilot shriek'd,
And fell down in a fit ;
The holy Hermit raised his eyes,
And pray'd where he did sit.

" I took the oars : the pilot's boy,
Who now doth crazy go,
Laugh'd loud and long, and all the while
His eyes went to and fro.
' Ha ! ha ! ' quoth he, ' full plain I see,
The Devil knows how to row.'

" And now, all in my own countree,
I stood on the firm land ! .
The Hermit stepp'd forth from the boat,
And scarcely he could stand.

" ' O, shrieve me, shrieve me, holy man ! '
The Hermit cross'd his brow.
' Say quick,' quoth he, ' I bid thee say—
What manner of man art thou ? '

" Forthwith this frame of mine was wrench'd
With a woeful agony,
Which forced me to begin my tale ;
And then it left me free.

" Since then at an uncertain hour,
That agony returns ;
And till my ghastly tale is told,
This heart within me burns.

" I pass, like night, from land to land ;
I have strange power of speech ;
That moment that his face I see,
I know the man that must hear me :
To him my tale I teach.

" What loud uproar bursts from that door !
The wedding-guests are there ;
But in the garden-bower the bride
And bride-maids singing are ;
And hark, the little vesper bell,
Which biddeth me to prayer !

" O Wedding-Guest ! this soul hath been
Alone on a wide wide sea :
So lonely 'twas, that God Himself
Scarce seemed there to be.

" O sweeter than the marriage-feast,
'Tis sweeter far to me,
To walk together to the kirk
With a goodly company !—

" To walk together to the kirk,
And all together pray,
While each to his great Father bends,
Old men, and babes, and loving friends,
And youths and maidens gay !

" Farewell, farewell ! but this I tell
To thee, thou Wedding-Guest !
He prayeth well, who loveth well
Both man and bird and beast.

" He prayeth best, who loveth best
All things both great and small :
For the dear God who loveth us,
He made and loveth all."

The Mariner, whose eye is bright,
Whose beard with age is hoar,
Is gone ; and now the Wedding-Guest
Turned from the bridegroom's door.

He went like one that hath been stunn'd,
And is of sense forlorn :
A sadder and a wiser man,
He rose the morrow morn.

S. T. COLERIDGE.

THE WELL
OF
Sᵗ KEYNE

A WELL there is in the west country,
    And a clearer one never was seen ;
There is not a wife in the west country
    But has heard of the Well of St Keyne.

An oak and an elm tree stand beside,
    And behind doth an ash-tree grow,
And a willow from the bank above
    Droops to the water below.

A traveller came to the Well of St Keyne,
        Joyfully he drew nigh,
     For from cock-crow he had been
       travelling,
     And there was not a cloud in the
       sky.

     He drank of the water so cool and
       clear,
     For thirsty and hot was he,
  And he sat down upon the bank
      Under the willow tree.

There came a man from the house hard by
  At the Well to fill his pail ;
On the Well-side he rested it,
  And he bade the Stranger hail.

"Now art thou a bachelor, Stranger?" quoth
    he,
  " For an if thou hast a wife,
The happiest draught thou hast drank this day
  That ever thou didst in thy life.

" Or has thy good woman, if one thou hast,
  Ever here in Cornwall been?
For an if she have, I'll venture my life
  She has drank of the Well of St Keyne."

"I have left a good woman who never was
    here,"
  The Stranger he made reply,
" But that my draught should be better for that,
  I pray you answer me why."

" St Keyne," quoth the Cornish-man, " many
    a time
  Drank of this crystal Well,
And before the Angel summon'd her,
  She laid on the water a spell.

" If the husband of this gifted Well
  Shall drink before his wife,
A happy man thenceforth is he,
  For he shall be master for life.

" But if the wife should drink of it first,
    God help the husband then ! "
The stranger stoopt to the Well of St Keyne,
    And drank of the water again.

"You drank of the Well, I warrant, betimes ? "
    He to the Cornish-man said :
But the Cornish-man smiled as the Stranger
        spake,
    And sheepishly shook his head.

" I hasten'd as soon as the wedding was done,
    And left my wife in the porch ;
But i' faith she had been wiser than me,
    For she took a bottle to Church."

R. SOUTHEY.

WESTBURY, 1798.

❧ Alonzo the Brave
and Fair Imogine ❧

A WARRIOR so bold and a virgin so bright
  Conversed, as they sat on the green ;
They gazed on each other with tender delight :
Alonzo the Brave was the name of the knight,
  The maid's was the Fair Imogine.

" And, oh ! " said the youth, " since to-morrow
    I go
To fight in a far-distant land,
Your tears for my absence soon leaving to flow,
Some other will court you, and you will bestow
  On a wealthier suitor your hand."

" Oh ! hush these suspicions," Fair Imogine said,
  " Offensive to love and to me !
For if you be living, or if you be dead,
I swear by the Virgin, that none in your stead
  Shall husband of Imogine be.

" And if e'er for another my heart should decide,
  Forgetting Alonzo the Brave,
God grant, that, to punish my falsehood and
      pride,
Your ghost at the marriage may sit by my side,
May tax me with perjury, claim me as bride,
  And bear me away to the grave ! "

To Palestine hasten'd the hero so bold ;
   His love she lamented him sore :
But scarce had a twelvemonth elapsed, when
     behold,
A baron all cover'd with jewels and gold
   Arrived at fair Imogine's door.

His treasure, his presents, his spacious domain
   Soon made her untrue to her vows :
He dazzled her eyes, he bewilder'd her brain,
He caught her affections so light and so vain,
   And carried her home as his spouse.

And now had the marriage been bless'd by the
     priest ;
   The revelry now was begun ;
The tables they groan'd with the weight of the
     feast,
Nor yet had the laughter and merriment ceased,
   When the bell of the castle toll'd—" one ! "

Then first with amazement fair Imogine found
   That a stranger was placed by her side :
His air was terrific ; he uttered no sound ;
He spoke not, he moved not, he look'd not
     around,
   But earnestly gazed on the bride.

His vizor was closed, and gigantic his height,
    His armour was sable to view :
All pleasure and laughter were hush'd at his
        sight,
The dogs, as they eyed him, drew back in
        affright,
    The lights in the chamber burnt blue!

His presence all bosoms appear'd to dismay ;
    The guests sat in silence and fear :
At length spoke the bride, while she trembled :—
        " I pray,
Sir knight, that your helmet aside you would lay,
    And deign to partake of our cheer."

The lady is silent ; the stranger complies ;
    His vizor he slowly unclosed :
Oh ! then what a sight met Fair Imogine's eyes!
What words can express her dismay and surprise,
    When a skeleton's head was exposed !

All present then utter'd a terrified shout ;
    All turn'd with disgust from the scene.
The worms they crept in, and the worms they
        crept out,
And sported his eyes and his temples about,
    While the spectre address'd Imogine :

"Behold me, thou false one! behold me!" he
 cried ;
 "Remember Alonzo the Brave!
God grants that, to punish thy falsehood and
 pride,
My ghost at thy marriage should sit by thy side,
Should tax thee with perjury, claim thee as
 bride,
 And bear thee away to the grave!"

Thus saying, his arms round the lady he wound,
 While loudly she shriek'd in dismay,
Then sank with his prey through the wide-
 yawning ground :
Nor ever again was Fair Imogine found,
 Or the spectre who bore her away.

Not long lived the Baron : and none since that
 time
 To inhabit the castle presume ;
For chronicles tell, that, by order sublime,
There Imogine suffers the pain of her crime,
 And mourns her deplorable doom.

At midnight four times in each year does her
 sprite,
 When mortals in slumber are bound,
Array'd in her bridal apparel of white,
Appear in the hall with the skeleton-knight,
 And shriek as he whirls her around.

While they drink out of skulls newly torn from
    the grave,
Dancing round them pale spectres are seen :
Their liquor is blood, and this horrible stave
They howl :—" To the health of Alonzo the
    Brave,
And his consort, the False Imogine ! "

M. G. Lewis (The Monk).

∽ Lord Ullin's Daughter ∾

A chieftain, to the Highlands bound,
    Cries, " Boatman, do not tarry !
And I'll give thee a silver pound
    To row us o'er the ferry."—

" Now who be ye would cross Lochgyle,
    This dark and stormy water ? "
" O, I'm the chief of Ulva's isle,
    And this Lord Ullin's daughter.—

" And fast before her father's men
    Three days we've fled together,
For should he find us in the glen,
    My blood would stain the heather.

" His horsemen hard behind us ride ;
    Should they our steps discover,
Then who will cheer my bonny bride
    When they have slain her lover ? "—

Out spoke the hardy Highland wight,
  " I'll go, my chief—I'm ready :—
It is not for your silver bright ;
  But for your winsome lady :

" And by my word ! the bonny bird
  In danger shall not tarry ;
So though the waves are raging white,
  I'll row you o'er the ferry."—

By this the storm grew loud apace,
  The water-wraith was shrieking ;
And in the scowl of Heaven each face
  Grew dark as they were speaking.

But still as wilder blew the wind,
  And as the night grew drearer,
Adown the glen rode armed men,
  Their trampling sounded nearer.—

" O haste thee, haste ! " the lady cries,
  " Though tempests round us gather ;
I'll meet the raging of the skies,
  But not an angry father."—

The boat has left a stormy land,
  A stormy sea before her,—
When, oh ! too strong for human hand,
  The tempest gather'd o'er her.

III.   K

And still they row'd amidst the roar
  Of waters fast prevailing ;
Lord Ullin reach'd that fatal shore,
  His wrath was changed to wailing.—

For sore dismay'd, through storm and shade,
  His child he did discover ;—
One lovely hand she stretch'd for aid,
  And one was round her lover.

"Come back ! come back !" he cried in grief,
  " Across this stormy water ;
And I'll forgive your Highland chief,
  My daughter !—Oh my daughter !"—

'Twas vain :—the loud waves lash'd the shore,
  Return or aid preventing :—
The waters wild went o'er his child,
  And he was left lamenting.

T. CAMPBELL.

✽ The Battle of the Baltic ✽
1809.

I.

OF Nelson and the North,
Sing the glorious day's renown,
When to battle fierce came forth
All the might of Denmark's crown,

And her arms along the deep proudly shone ;
By each gun the lighted brand,
In a bold determined hand,
And the Prince of all the land
Led them on.—

II.

Like leviathans afloat,
Lay their bulwarks on the brine,
While the sign of battle flew
On the lofty British line :
It was ten of April morn by the chime :
As they drifted on their path,
There was silence deep as death ;
And the boldest held his breath
For a time.—

III

But the might of England flush'd
To anticipate the scene ;
And her van the fleeter rush'd
O'er the deadly space between.
" Hearts of oak ! " our captains cried ; when
        each gun
From its adamantine lips
Spread a death-shade round the ships,
Like the hurricane eclipse
Of the sun.

IV.

Again! again! again!
And the havoc did not slack,
Till a feeble cheer the Dane
To our cheering sent us back ;—
Their shots along the deep slowly boom :—
Then ceased—and all is wail,
As they strike the shatter'd sail,
Or, in conflagration pale,
Light the gloom.—

V.

Out spoke the victor then,
As he hail'd them o'er the wave :
" Ye are brothers ! ye are men !
And we conquer but to save ;—
So peace instead of death let us bring ;
But yield, proud foe, thy fleet,
With the crews, at England's feet,
And make submission meet
To our King."—

VI.

Then Denmark bless'd our chief,
That he gave her wounds repose ;
And the sounds of joy and grief
From her people wildly rose,

As death withdrew his shades from the day.
While the sun look'd smiling bright
O'er a wide and woeful sight,
Where the fires of funeral light
Died away.

VII.

Now joy, old England, raise !
For the tidings of thy might,
By the festal cities' blaze,
While the wine-cup shines in light ;
And yet amidst that joy and uproar,
Let us think of them that sleep,
Full many a fathom deep,
By thy wild and stormy steep,
Elsinore !

VIII.

Brave hearts ! to Britain's pride
Once so faithful and so true,
On the deck of fame that died,—
With the gallant good Riou ;
Soft sigh the winds of heaven o'er their grave !
While the billow mournful rolls,
And the mermaid's song condoles,
Singing glory to the souls
Of the brave !—

T. CAMPBELL.

The War-Song of Dinas Vawr

The mountain sheep are sweeter,
But the valley sheep are fatter;
We therefore deemed it meeter
To carry off the latter.
We made an expedition;
We met an host and quelled it;
We forced a strong position,
And killed·the men who held it.

On Dyfed's richest valley,
Where herds of kine were browsing,
We made a mighty sally,
To furnish our carousing.
Fierce warriors rushed to meet us;
We met them, and o'erthrew them:
They struggled hard to beat us;
But we conquered them, and slew them.

As we drove our prize at leisure,
The king marched forth to catch us:
His rage surpassed all measure,
But his people could not match us.
He fled to his hall-pillars;
And, ere our force we led off,
Some sacked his house and cellars,
While others cut his head off.

We there, in strife bewildering,
Spilt blood enough to swim in :
We orphaned many children,
And widowed many women.
The eagles and the ravens
We glutted with our foemen ;
The heroes and the cravens,
The spearmen and the bowmen.

We brought away from battle,
And much their land bemoaned them,
Two thousand head of cattle,
And the head of him who owned them :
Ednyfed, King of Dyfed,
His head was borne before us ;
His wine and beasts supplied our feasts,
And his overthrow, our chorus.

T. L. Peacock.

The Cauldron

of

Ceridwen

THE sage Ceridwen was the wife
Of Tegid Voël, of Pemble Mere :
Two children blest their wedded life,
Morvran and Creirwy, fair and dear :
Morvran, a son of peerless worth,
And Creirwy, loveliest nymph of earth :
But one more son Ceridwen bare,
As foul as they before were fair.

She strove to make Avagddu wise ;
She knew he never could be fair :
And, studying magic mysteries,
She gathered plants of virtue rare :
She placed the gifted plants to steep
Within the magic cauldron deep,
Where they a year and day must boil,
Till three drops crown the matron's toil.

Nine damsels raised the mystic flame ;
Gwion the Little near it stood :
The while for simples roved the dame
Through tangled dell and pathless wood ;
And, when the year and day had past,
The dame within the cauldron cast
The consummating chaplet wild,
While Gwion held the hideous child.

But from the cauldron rose a smoke
That filled with darkness all the air :
When through its folds the torchlight broke,
Nor Gwion, nor the boy, was there.
The fire was dead, the cauldron cold,
And in it lay, in sleep unrolled,
Fair as the morning-star, a child,
That woke, and stretched its arms, and smiled.

What chanced her labours to destroy,
She never knew ; and sought in vain
If 'twere her own misshapen boy,
Or little Gwion, born again :
And, vext with doubt, the babe she rolled
In cloth of purple and of gold,
And in a coracle consigned
Its fortunes to the sea and wind.

The summer night was still and bright,
The summer moon was large and clear,
The frail bark, on the springtide's height,
Was floated into Elphin's weir.

The baby in his arms he raised :
His lovely spouse stood by, and gazed,
And, blessing it with gentle vow,
Cried " TALIESIN ! " " Radiant brow ! "

And I am he : and well I know
Ceridwen's power protects me still ;
And hence o'er hill and vale I go,
And sing, unharmed, whate'er I will.
She has for me Time's veil withdrawn :
The images of things long gone,
The shadows of the coming days,
Are present to my visioned gaze.

And I have heard the words of power,
By Ceirion's solitary lake,
That bid, at midnight's thrilling hour,
Eryri's hundred echoes wake.
I to Diganwy's towers have sped,
And now Caer Lleon's halls I tread,
Demanding justice, now, as then,
From Maelgon, most unjust of men.

T. L. PEACOCK.

Llyn-y-Dreiddiad-Vrawd

(*The Pool
of the
Diving Friar.*)

GWENWYNWYN withdrew from the feasts of his
    hall ;
He slept very little, he prayed not at all ;
He pondered, and wandered, and studied alone ;
And sought, night and day, the philosopher's
    stone.

He found it at length, and he made its first proof
By turning to gold all the lead of his roof :
Then he bought some magnanimous heroes, all
    fire,
Who lived but to smite and be smitten for hire.

With these, on the plains like a torrent he broke ;
He filled the whole country with flame and with
    smoke ;

He killed all the swine, and he broached all the
    wine ;
He drove off the sheep, and the beeves, and the
    kine.

He took castles and towns ; he cut short limbs
    and lives ;
He made orphans and widows of children and
    wives :
This course many years he triumphantly ran,
And did mischief enough to be called a great man.

When, at last, he had gained all for which he
    had striven,
He bethought him of buying a passport to heaven ;
Good and great as he was, yet he did not well
    know
How soon, or which way, his great spirit might
    go.

He sought the grey friars, who, beside a wild
    stream,
Refected their frames on a primitive scheme ;
The gravest and wisest Gwenwynwyn found out,
All lonely and ghostly, and angling for trout.

Below the white dash of a mighty cascade,
Where a pool of the stream a deep resting-place
    made,
And rock-rooted oaks stretched their branches
    on high,
The friar stood musing and throwing his fly.

To him said Gwenwynwyn, "Hold, father,
    here's store,
For the good of the church, and the good of the
    poor ; "
Then he gave him the stone ; but, ere more he
    could speak,
Wrath came on the friar, so holy and meek.

He had stretched forth his hand to receive the
    red gold,
And he thought himself mocked by Gwenwynwyn
    the Bold ;
And in scorn of the gift, and in rage at the
    giver,
He jerked it immediately into the river.

Gwenwynwyn, aghast, not a syllable spake ;
The philosopher's stone made a duck and a drake ;
Two systems of circles a moment were seen,
And the stream smoothed them off, as they
    never had been.

Gwenwynwyn regained, and uplifted, his voice :
" Oh friar, grey friar, full rash was thy choice ;
The stone, the good stone, which away thou
    hast thrown,
Was the stone of all stones, the philosopher's
    stone ! "

The friar looked pale, when his error he knew ;
The friar looked red, and the friar looked blue ;
And heels over head, from the point of a rock,
He plunged, without stopping to pull off his
    frock.

He dived very deep, but he dived all in vain,
The prize he had slighted he found not again :
Many times did the friar his diving renew,
And deeper and deeper the river still grew.

Gwenwynwyn gazed long, of his senses in doubt,
To see the grey friar a diver so stout :
Then sadly and slowly his castle he sought,
And left the friar diving, like dabchick distraught.

Gwenwynwyn fell sick with alarm and despite,
Died, and went to the devil, the very same night :
The magnanimous heroes he held in his pay
Sacked his castle, and marched with the plunder
    away.

No knell on the silence of midnight was rolled,
For the flight of the soul of Gwenwynwyn the
    Bold :
The brethren, unfeed, let the mighty ghost pass,
Without praying a prayer, or intoning a mass.

The friar haunted ever beside the dark stream ;
The philosopher's stone was his thought and his
    dream :

And day after day, ever head under heels
He dived all the time he could spare from his
    meals.

He dived, and he dived, to the end of his days,
As the peasants oft witnessed with fear and
    amaze :
The mad friar's diving-place long was their
    theme,
And no plummet can fathom that pool of the
    stream.

And still, when light clouds on the midnight
    winds ride,
If by moonlight you stray on the lone river-side,
The ghost of the friar may be seen diving there,
With head in the water, and heels in the air.

T. L. Peacock.

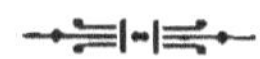

Willy

and Helen

"Wharefore sou'd ye talk o' love,
    Unless it be to pain us ?
Wharefore sou'd ye talk o' love
    Whan ye say the sea maun twain us ? "

"It's no because my love is light,
  Nor for your angry deddy,
It's a' to buy ye pearlins bright,
  An' to busk ye like a leddy."

"O, Willy ! I can caird an' spin,
  Sae ne'er can want for cleeding ;
And, gin I ha'e my Willy's heart,
  I ha'e a' the pearls I'm heedin'.

"Will it be time to praise this cheek,
  Whan years an' tears ha'e blench'd it ?
Will it be time to talk o' love
  Whan cauld an' care ha'e quench'd it ?"

He's laid ae han' aboot her waist,
  The ither's held to heaven ;
An' his luik was like the luik o' man
  Wha's heart in twa is riven.

.   .   .   .   .

The auld laird o' Knockdon is dead,
  There's few for him will sorrow ;
For Willy's steppit in his stead,
  But an' his comely marrow.

There's a cosy bield at yon burn fit,
  Wi' a bourtree at the en' o't ;
O, mony a day may it see yet
  Ere care or canker ken o't !

The lily leans out owre the brae,
  An' the rose leans owre the lily :
An' there the bonny twasome lay—
  Fair Helen an' her Willy.

HEW AINSLIE.

Sir Arthur and Lady Ann

SIR ARTHUR'S foot is on the sand,
  His boat wears in the wind ;
An' he's turned him to a fair foot page
  Who was standing him behind.

" Gae hame, gae hame, my bonny boy,
  An' glad your mither's e'e ;
I hae left anew to weep an' rue,
  Sae nane maun weep for thee.

" Take this unto my father's ha',
  An' tell him I maun speed ;
There's fifty men in chase o' me,
  An' a price upon my head.

" An' bear this to Dunellie's towers,
  Where my love Annie's gane ;
It is a lock o' my brown hair,
  Girt wi' the diamond stane."

" Dunellie he has daughters five,
  An' some o' them are fair,
Sae, how will I ken thy true love
  Amang sae mony there ?"

III.   L

" Ye'll ken her by her stately step
   As she gaes up the ha' ;
Ye'll ken her by the look o' love
   That peers out owre them a' ;

" Ye'll ken her by the braid o' goud
   That spreads owre her e'e bree ;
Ye'll ken her by the red, red cheek
   When ye name the name o' me.

" That cheek should lain on this breast-bane,
   Her hame should been my ha' ;
Our tree is bow'd—our flower is dow'd—
   Sir Arthur's an outlaw ! "

He sighed, an' turned him right about,
   Where the sea lay braid an' wide :
It's no to see his boony boat,
   But a watery cheek to hide.

The page has doff'd his feather'd cap,
   But an' his raven hair ;
An' out there came the yellow locks,
   Like swirls o' the gouden wair.

Syne he's undone his doublet clasp,
   Was o' the grass-green hue,
When, like a lily frae its leaf,
   A lady burst in view.

" Tell out thy errand now, Sir Knight,
   Wi' thy love tokens a' ;
If I e'er rin against my will,
   'Twill be at a lover's ca' ! "

Sir Arthur's turned him round about,
   E'en as the lady spak' ;
An' thrice he dighted his dim e'e,
   An' thrice he steppit back.

But ae blink o' her bonny e'e,
  · Out spake his Lady Ann ;
An' he's catch'd her by the waist sae sma',
   Wi' the grip o' a drowning man.

"O ! Lady Ann, thy bed's been hard,
   When I thought it the down ;
O ! Lady Ann, thy love's been deep,
   When I thought it was flown.

" I've met my love in the greenwood,
   My foe on the brown hill ;
But I ne'er met wi' aught before
   I liked sae weel, an' ill.

"O I could make a Queen o' thee,
   An' it would be my pride ;
But, Lady Ann, it's no for thee
   To be an outlaw's bride."

" Hae I left kith an' kin, Sir Knight,
　　To turn about and rue ?
Hae I shar'd win' an' weet wi' thee,
　　That I should leave thee noo ?

" 'There's gowd an' siller in this han'
　　Will buy us mony a rigg ;
There's pearlings in the other han'
　　A stately tower to bigg.

" Tho' thou'rt an outlaw frae this lan',
　　The warl's braid an' wide ;
Make room, make room, my merry men,
　　For young Sir Arthur's bride !"

　　　　　　　　　HEW AINSLIE.

❧ The Fugitives ❧

I.

THE waters are flashing,
The white hail is dashing,
The lightnings are glancing,
The hoar-spray is dancing—
　　　　Away !

The whirlwind is rolling,
The thunder is tolling,
The forest is swinging,
The minster bells ringing—
　　　　Come away !

The earth is like ocean,
Wreck-strewn and in motion :
Bird, beast, man and worm
Have crept out of the storm—
    Come away !

II.

" Our boat has one sail,
And the helmsman is pale ;—
A bold pilot I trow,
Who shall follow us now,"—
    Shouted he—

And she cried : " Ply the oar !
Put off gaily from shore ! "—
As she spoke, bolts of death
Mixed with hail, specked their path
    O'er the sea.

And from isle, tower and rock,
The blue beacon cloud broke,
And though dumb in the blast,
The red cannon flashed fast
    From the lee.

III.

" And fear'st thou, and fear'st thou ?
And see'st thou, and hear'st thou ?
And drive we not free
O'er the terrible sea,
    I and thou ? "

One boat-cloak did cover
The loved and the lover—
Their blood beats one measure,
They murmur proud pleasure
    Soft and low ;—

While around the lashed ocean,
Like mountains in motion,
Is withdrawn and uplifted,
Sunk, shattered and shifted
    To and fro.

IV.

In the court of the fortress
Beside the pale portress,
Like a bloodhound well beaten
The bridegroom stands, eaten
    By shame ;

On the topmost watch-turret,
As a death-boding spirit,
Stands the gray tyrant father,
To his voice the mad weather
    Seems tame ;

And with curses as wild
As e'er clung to child,
He devotes to the blast
The best, loveliest, and last
    Of his name !

P. B. SHELLEY.

<h1 style="text-align:center">La
Belle Dame
Sans
Merci</h1>

I.

" O what can ail thee, knight-at-arms,
   Alone and palely loitering ?
The sedge has wither'd from the lake,
   And no birds sing.

II.

" O what can ail thee, knight-at-arms,
   So haggard and so woe-begone ?
The squirrel's granary is full,
   And the harvest's done.

III.

" I see a lily on thy brow
   With anguish moist and fever dew ;
And on thy cheek a fading rose
   Fast withereth too."

IV.

" I met a lady in the meads,
    Full beautiful—a faery's child,
Her hair was long, her foot was light,
    And her eyes were wild.

V.

" I made a garland for her head,
    And bracelets too, and fragrant zone ;
She look'd at me as she did love,
    And made sweet moan.

VI.

" I set her on my pacing steed,
    And nothing else saw all day long,
For sideways would she bend, and sing
    A faery's song.

VII.

" She found me roots of relish sweet,
    And honey wild, and manna dew,
And sure in language strange she said,
    ' I love thee true.'

VIII.

" She took me to her elfin grot,
    And there she wept and sigh'd full sore,
And there I shut her wild wild eyes
    With kisses four.

IX.

" And there she lulled me asleep,
  And there I dream'd—ah ! woe betide !
The latest dream I ever dream'd
  On the cold hill's side.

X.

" I saw pale kings and princes too,
  Pale warriors, death-pale were they all ;
Who cry'd—' La belle Dame sans Merci
  Hath thee in thrall ! '

XI.

" I saw their starv'd lips in the gloam,
  With horrid warning gaped wide,
And I awoke and found me here,
  On the cold hill's side.

XII.

" And this is why I sojourn here,
  Alone and palely loitering,
Though the sedge is withered from the lake,
  And no birds sing."

J. KEATS.

≈ The Rose
and the Fair Lily ≈

The Earlsburn Glen is gay and green,
The Earlsburn water cleir,
And blythely blume on Earlsburn bank
The broom and eke the brier!

Twa sisters gaed up Earlsburn Glen—
Twa maidens bricht o' blee—
The tane she was the Rose sae red,
The tither the fair Lilye!

" Ye mauna droop and dwyne, sister "—
Said Ròse to fair Lilye—
" Yer heart ye mauna brek, sister—
For ane that's ower the sea ;

" The vows we sillie maidens hear
Frae wild and wilfu' man,
Are as the words the waves wash out
When traced upon the san'."

" I mauna think yer speech is sooth,"
Saft answered the Lilye ;
" I winna dout mine ain gude knicht
Tho' he's ayont the sea ! "

Then scornfully the Rose sae red
   Spake to the puir Lilye—
" The vows he feigned at thy bouir door,
   He plicht in mine to me ! "

" I'll hame and spread the sheets, sister,
   And deck my bed sae hie—
The bed sae wide made for a bride
 . For I think I sune sal die !

" Your weird I sal na be, sister,
   As mine I fear ye've bin—
Your luve I wil na cross, sister,
   It were a mortal sin ! "

Earlsburn Glen is green to see,
   Earlsburn water cleir—
Of the siller birk in Earlsburn Wood
   They framit the maiden's bier !

There's a lonely dame in a gudely bouir,
   She never lifts an ee—
That dame was ance the Rose sae red,
   She is now a pale Lilye.

A knicht aft looks frae his turret tall,
   Where the kirk-yaird grass grows green ;
He wonne the weed and lost the flouir,
   And grief aye dims his een.

At noon of nicht, in the moonshine bricht,
  The warrior kneels in prayer—
He prays wi' his face to the auld kirk-yaird,
  And wishes he were there !
                    W. MOTHERWELL.

≈ Faithless Sally Brown ≈

YOUNG Ben he was a nice young man,
  A carpenter by trade ;
And he fell in love with Sally Brown,
  That was a lady's maid.

But as they fetched a walk one day,
  They met a press-gang crew ;
And Sally she did faint away,
  Whilst Ben he was brought to.

The Boatswain swore with wicked words,
  Enough to shock a saint,
That though she did seem in a fit,
  'Twas nothing but a feint.

" Come, girl," said he, " hold up your head,
  He'll be as good as me ;
For when your swain is in our boat,
  A boatswain he will be."

So when they'd made their game of her,
    And taken off her elf,
She roused, and found she only was
    A coming to herself.

" And is he gone, and is he gone ? "
    She cried, and wept outright :
" Then I will to the water side,
    And see him out of sight."

A waterman came up to her,
    " Now, young woman," said he,
" If you weep on so, you will make
    Eye-water in the sea."

" Alas ! they've taken my beau, Ben,
    To sail with old Benbow ; "
And her woe began to run afresh,
    As if she'd said, Gee woe !

Says he, " They've only taken him
    To the Tender-ship, you see ; "
" The Tender-ship," cried Sally Brown,
    " What a hard-ship that must be !

" Oh ! would I were a mermaid now,
    For then I'd follow him ;
But oh !—I'm not a fish-woman,
    And so I cannot swim.

" Alas ! I was not born beneath
  The Virgin and the Scales,
So I must curse my cruel stars,
  And walk about in Wales."

Now Ben had sailed to many a place
  That's underneath the world ;
But in two years the ship came home,
  And all her sails were furled.

But when he called on Sally Brown,
  To see how she went on,
He found she'd got another Ben,
  Whose Christian name was John.

"O Sally Brown, O Sally Brown,
  How could you serve me so,
I've met with many a breeze before,
  But never such a blow."

Then reading on his 'bacco box,
  He heaved a bitter sigh,
And then began to eye his pipe,
  And then to pipe his eye.

And then he tried to sing " All's Well,"
  But could not though he tried :
His head was turned, and so he chewed
  His pigtail till he died.

His death, which happened in his berth,
    At forty-odd befell :
They went and told the sexton, and
    The sexton toll'd the bell.

T. Hood.

Faithless Nelly Gray

Ben Battle was a soldier bold,
    And used to war's alarms ;
But a cannon-ball took off his legs,
    So he laid down his arms !

Now as they bore him off the field,
    Said he, " Let others shoot,
For here I leave my second leg,
    And the Forty-second Foot ! "

The army-surgeons made him limbs :
    Said he,—" They're only pegs :
But there's as wooden members quite
    As represent my legs ! "

Now Ben he loved a pretty maid,
    Her name was Nelly Gray ;
So he went to pay her his devours,
    When he'd devoured his pay !

But when he called on Nelly Gray,
   She made him quite a scoff;
And when she saw his wooden legs,
   Began to take them off!

" Oh, Nelly Gray! Oh, Nelly Gray!
   Is this your love so warm?
The love that loves a scarlet coat,
   Should be more uniform!"

She said, "I loved a soldier once,
   For he was blithe and brave;
But I will never have a man
   With both legs in the grave!

" Before you had those timber toes,
   Your love I did allow,
But then, you know, you stand upon
   Another footing now!"

" Oh, Nelly Gray! Oh, Nelly Gray!
   For all your jeering speeches,
At duty's call, I left my legs
   In Badajos's *breaches!*"

" Why then," said she, " you've lost the feet
   Of legs in war's alarms,
And now you cannot wear your shoes
   Upon you feats of arms!"

III.   M

" Oh, false and fickle Nelly Gray !
    I know why you refuse :—
Though I've no feet—some other man
    Is standing in my shoes !

" I wish I ne'er had seen your face ;
    But now a long farewell !
For you will be my death ;—alas !
    You will not be my *Nell !* "

Now when he went from Nelly Gray,
    His heart so heavy got—
And life was such a burthen grown,
    It made him take a knot !

So round his melancholy neck
    A rope he did entwine,
And, for his second time in life,
    Enlisted in the Line !

One end he tied around a beam,
    And then removed his pegs,
And, as his legs were off,—of course,
    He soon was off his legs !

And there he hung, till he was dead
    As any nail in town,—
For though distress had cut him up,
    It could not cut him down !

A dozen men sat on his corpse,
    To find out why he died—
And they buried Ben in four cross roads,
    With a *stake* in his inside !

T. Hood.

The Dream
of Eugene Aram

'Twas in the prime of summer time,
    An evening calm and cool,
And four-and-twenty happy boys
    Came bounding out of school :
There were some that ran and some that leapt,
    Like troutlets in a pool.

Away they sped with gamesome minds,
    And souls untouched by sin ;
To a level mead they came, and there
    They drave the wickets in :
Pleasantly shone the setting sun
    Over the town of Lynn.

Like sportive deer they coursed about,
    And shouted as they ran,—
Turning to mirth all things of earth,
    As only boyhood can ;
But the Usher sat remote from all,
    A melancholy man !

His hat was off, his vest apart,
　　To catch heaven's blessed breeze ;
For a burning thought was in his brow,
　　And his bosom ill at ease :
So he leaned his head on his hands, and read
　　The book upon his knees !

Leaf after leaf he turned it o'er,
　　Nor ever glanced aside,
For the peace of his soul he read that book
　　In the golden eventide :
Much study had made him very lean,
　　And pale, and leaden-eyed.

At last he shut the pond'rous tome,
　　With a fast and fervent grasp
He strained the dusky covers close,
　　And fixed the brazen hasp :
" Oh, God ! could I so close my mind,
　　And clasp it with a clasp ! "

Then leaping on his feet upright,
　　Some moody turns he took,—
Now up the mead, then down the mead,
　　And past a shady nook,—
And lo ! he saw a little boy
　　That pored upon a book.

" My gentle lad, what is't you read—
　　Romance or fairy fable ?

Or is it some historic page,
    Of kings and crown unstable ? "
The young boy gave an upward glance,—
    " It is ' The Death of Abel.' "

The Usher took six hasty strides,
    As smit with sudden pain,—
Six hasty strides beyond the place,
    Then slowly back again ;
And down he sat beside the lad,
    And talked with him of Cain ;

And, long since then, of bloody men,
    Whose deeds tradition saves ;
Of lonely folk cut off unseen,
    And hid in sudden graves ;
Of horrid stabs, in groves forlorn,
    And murders done in caves ;

And how the sprites of injured men
    Shriek upward from the sod,—
Aye, how the ghostly hand will point
    To show the burial clod ;
And unknown facts of guilty acts
    Are seen in dreams from God !

He told how murderers walk the earth
    Beneath the curse of Cain—
With crimson clouds before their eyes,
    And flames about their brain :
For blood has left upon their souls
    Its everlasting stain !

" And well," quoth he, " I know, for truth,
    Their pangs must be extreme,—
Woe, woe, unutterable woe,—
    Who spill life's sacred stream !
For why? Methought, last night, I wrought
    A murder, in my dream !

"One that had never done me wrong—
    A feeble man, and old ;
I led him to a lonely field,—
    The moon shone clear and cold :
Now here, said I, this man shall die,
    And I will have his gold !

" Two sudden blows with a ragged stick,
    And one with a heavy stone,
One hurried gash with a hasty knife,—
    And then the deed was done :
There was nothing lying at my foot
    But lifeless flesh and bone !

" Nothing but lifeless flesh and bone,
    That could not do me ill ;
And yet I feared him all the more,
    For lying there so still :
There was a manhood in his look,
    That murder could not kill !

" And lo ! the universal air
    Seemed lit with ghastly flame ;—

Ten thousand thousand dreadful eyes
    Were looking down in blame :
I took the dead man by his hand,
    And called upon his name !

" O God ! it made me quake to see
    Such sense within the slain !
But when I touched the lifeless clay,
    The blood gushed out amain !
For every clot, a burning spot
    Was scorching in my brain !

" My head was like an ardent coal,
    My heart as solid ice ;
My wretched, wretched soul, I knew,
    Was at the Devil's price :
A dozen times I groaned ; the dead
    Had never groaned but twice !

" And now, from forth the frowning sky,
    From the Heaven's topmost height,
I heard a voice—the awful voice
    Of the blood-avenging sprite :—
' Thou guilty man ! take up thy dead
    And hide it from my sight ! '

" I took the dreary body up,
    And cast it in a stream,—
A sluggish water, black as ink,
    The depth was so extreme :—

My gentle Boy, remember this
    Is nothing but a dream!

" Down went the corse with a hollow plunge,
    And vanished in the pool!
Anon I cleansed my bloody hands,
    And washed my forehead cool,
And sat among the urchins young,
    That evening in the school.

" Oh, Heaven! to think of their white souls,
    And mine so black and grim!
I could not share in childish prayer,
    Nor join in Evening Hymn :
Like a Devil of the Pit I seemed
    'Mid holy Cherubim!

" And peace went with them, one and all,
    And each calm pillow spread ;
But Guilt was my grim Chamberlain
    That lighted me to bed ;
And drew my midnight curtains round,
    With fingers bloody red!

" All night I lay in agony,
    In anguish dark and deep ;
My fevered eyes I dared not close,
    But stared aghast at Sleep :
For Sin had rendered unto her
    The keys of Hell to keep!

" All night I lay in agony,
      From weary chime to chime,
With one besetting horrid hint,
      That racked me all the time ;
A mighty yearning, like the first
      Fierce impulse unto crime !

" One stern tyrannic thought, that made
      All other thoughts its slave ;
Stronger and stronger every pulse
      Did that temptation crave,—
Still urging me to go and see
      The Dead Man in his grave !

" Heavily I rose up, as soon
      As light was in the sky,
And sought the black accursèd pool
      With a wild misgiving eye ;
And I saw the Dead in the river bed,
      For the faithless stream was dry.

" Merrily rose the lark, and shook
      The dewdrop from its wing ;
But I never marked its morning flight,
      I never heard it sing :
For I was stooping once again
      Under the horrid thing.

" With breathless speed, like a soul in
        chase,
      I took him up and ran ; —

There was no time to dig a grave
　　Before the day began :
In a lonesome wood, with heaps of leaves,
　　I hid the murdered man!

" And all that day I read in school,
　　But my thought was other-where ;
As soon as the mid-day task was done,
　　In secret I was there :
And a mighty wind had swept the leaves,
　　And still the corse was bare !

" Then down I cast me on my face,
　　And first began to weep,
For I knew my secret then was one
　　That earth refused to keep :
Or land or sea, though he should be
　　Ten thousand fathoms deep.

" So wills the fierce avenging Sprite,
　　Till blood for blood atones !
Ay, though he's buried in a cave,
　　And trodden down with stones,
And years have rotted off his flesh,—
　　The world shall see his bones !

" Oh, God ! that horrid, horrid dream
　　Besets me now awake !
Again—again, with dizzy brain,
　　The human life I take ;
And my red right hand grows raging hot,
　　Like Cranmer's at the stake.

" And still no peace for the restless clay,
  Will wave or mould allow ;
The horrid thing pursues my soul,—
  It stands before me now ! "
The fearful Boy looked up, and saw
  Huge drops upon his brow.

That very night, while gentle sleep
    The urchin eyelids kissed,
Two stern-faced men set out from Lynn,
    Through the cold and heavy mist ;
And Eugene Aram walked between,
    With gyves upon his wrist.
                              T. Hood.

————

The Voyage with the Nautilus

I MADE myself a little boat,
    As trim as trim could be ;
I made it of a great pearl shell
    Found in the Indian Sea.

I made my masts of wild sea-rush
    That grew on a secret shore,
And the scarlet plume of the halcyon
    Was the pleasant flag I bore.

For my sails I took the butterfly's wings ;
    For my ropes the spider's line ;
And that mariner old, the Nautilus,
    To steer me over the brine.

For he had sailed six thousand years,
    And knew each isle and bay ;
And I thought that we, in my little boat,
    Could merrily steer away.

The stores I took were plentiful :
  The dew as it sweetly fell ;
And the honey that was hoarded up
  In the wild bee's summer cell.

" Now steer away, thou helmsman good,
  Over the waters free ;
To the charmèd Isle of the Seven Kings,
  That lies in the midmost sea."

He spread the sail, he took the helm ;
  And, long ere ever I wist,
We had sailed a league, we had reached the isle
  That lay in the golden mist.

The charmèd Isle of the Seven Kings,
  'Tis a place of wondrous spell ;
And all that happed unto me there
  In a printed book I'll tell.

Said I, one day, to the Nautilus,
  As we stood on the strand,
" Unmoor my ship, thou helmsman good,
  And steer me back to land ;

" For my mother, I know, is sick at heart,
  And longs my face to see.
What ails thee now, thou Nautilus ?
  Art slow to sail with me ?
Up ! do my will ; the wind is fresh,
  So set the vessel free."

He turned the helm ; away we sailed
   Towards the setting sun :
The flying-fish were swift of wing,
   But we outsped each one.

And on we went for seven days,
   Seven days without a night ;
We followed the sun still on and on,
   In the glow of his setting light.

Down and down went the setting sun,
   And down and down went we ;
'Twas a splendid sail for seven days
   On a smooth descending sea.

On a smooth, descending sea we sailed,
   Nor breeze the water curled :
My brain grew sick, for I saw we sailed
   On the down-hill of the world.

" Good friend," said I to the Nautilus,
   " Can this the right course be ?
And shall we come again to land ? "
   But answer none made he ;
And I saw a laugh in his fishy eye
   As he turned it up to me.

So on we went ; but soon I heard
   A sound as when winds blow,
And waters wild are tumbled down
   Into a gulf below.

And on and on flew the little bark,
    As a fiend her course did urge ;
And I saw, in a moment, we must hang
    Upon the ocean's verge.

I snatched down the sails, I snapped the ropes,
    I broke the masts in twain ;
But on flew the bark and 'gainst the rocks
    Like a living thing did strain.

" Thou'st steered us wrong, thou helmsman
        vile ! "
    Said I to the Nautilus bold ;
" We shall down the gulf ; we're dead men
        both !
    Dost know the course we hold ? "

I seized the helm with a sudden jerk,
    And we wheeled round like a bird ;
But I saw the Gulf of Eternity,
    And the tideless waves I heard.

" Good master," said the Nautilus,
    " I thought you might desire
To have some wondrous thing to tell
    Beside your mother's fire.

" What's sailing on a summer sea ?
    As well sail on a pool ;
Oh, but I know a thousand things
    That are wild and beautiful !

" And if you wish to see them now,
  You've but to say the word."
" Have done ! " said I to the Nautilus,
  " Or I'll throw thee overboard.

" Have done ! " said I, " thou mariner old,
  And steer me back to land."
No other word spake the Nautilus,
  But took the helm in hand.

I looked up to the lady moon,
  She was like a glow-worm's spark ;
And never a star shone down to us
  Through the sky so high and dark.

We had no mast, we had no ropes,
  And every sail was rent ;
And the stores I brought from the charmèd
    isle
  In the seven days' sail were spent.

But the Nautilus was a patient thing,
  And steered with all his might
On the up-hill sea ; and he never slept,
  But kept the course aright.

And for thrice seven nights we sailed and
    sailed ;
  At length I saw the bay
Where I built my ship, and my mother's house
  'Mid the green hills where it lay.

III.   N

> " Farewell ! " said I to the Nautilus,
>   And leaped upon the shore ;
> " Thou art a skilful mariner,
>   But I'll sail with thee no more ! "
>
>   M. Howitt.

↜ The Doom-Well
of St Madron ↞

"Plunge thy right hand in St Madron's spring,
If true to its troth be the palm you bring :
But if a false sigil thy fingers bear,
Lay them the rather on the burning share."

Loud laughed King Arthur when-as he heard
That solemn friar his boding word :
And blithely he sware as a king he may,
"We tryst for St Madron's at break of day."

"Now horse and hattock, both but and ben,"
Was the cry at Lauds, with Dundagel men ;
And forth they pricked upon Routorr side,
As goodly a raid as a king could ride.

Proud Gwennivar rode like a queen of the land,
With page and with squire at her bridle hand ;
And the twice six knights of the stony ring,
They girded and guarded their Cornish king.

Then they halted their steeds at St Madron's cell :
And they stood by the monk of the cloistered
    well ;
" Now off with your gauntlets," King Arthur he
    cried,
" And glory or shame for our Tamar side."

'Twere sooth to sing how Sir Gauvain smiled,
When he grasped the waters so soft and mild ;
How Sir Lancelot dashed the glistening spray
O'er the rugged beard of the rough Sir Kay.

Sir Bevis he touched and he found no fear :
'Twas a *bénitée* stoup to Sir Belvidere,
Now the fountain flashed o'er King Arthur's
    Queen
Say, Cornish dames, for ye guess the scene.

" Now rede me my riddle, Sir Mordred, I pray,
My kinsman, mine ancient, my *bien-aimé* ;
Now rede me my riddle, and rede it aright,
Art thou traitorous knave or my trusty knight ? "

He plunged his right arm in the judgment
    well,
It bubbled and boiled like a cauldron of hell :
He drew and he lifted his quivering limb,
Ha ! Sir Judas, how Madron had sodden him.

Now let Uter Pendragon do what he can,
Still the Tamar river will run as it ran :
Let king or let kaiser be fond or be fell,
Ye may harowe their troth in St Madron's well.

R. S. HAWKER.

A KNIGHT of gallant deeds
    And a young page at his side,
From the holy war in Palestine
    Did slow and thoughtful ride,
As each were a palmer and told for beads
    The dews of the eventide.

" O young page," said the knight,
    " A noble page art thou !
Thou fearest not to steep in blood
    The curls upon thy brow ;
And once in the tent, and twice in the fight,
    Didst ward me a mortal blow."

"O brave knight," said the page,
  "Or ere we hither came,
We talked in tent, we talked in field,
  Of the bloody battle-game ;
But here, below this greenwood bough,
  I cannot speak the same.

" Our troop is far behind,
  The woodland calm is new ;
Our steeds, with slow grass-muffled hoofs,
  Tread deep the shadows through ;
And, in my mind, some blessing kind
  Is dropping with the dew.

" The woodland calm is pure—
  I cannot choose but have
A thought from these, o' the beechen trees,
  Which in our England wave,
And of the little finches fine
Which sang there while in Palestine
  The warrior-hilt we drave.

" Methinks, a moment gone,
  I heard my mother pray !
I heard, sir knight, the prayer for me
  Wherein she passed away ;
And I know the heavens are leaning down
  To hear what I shall say."

The page spake calm and high,
    As of no mean degree ;
Perhaps he felt in nature's broad
    Full heart, his own was free :
And the knight looked up to his lifted eye,
    Then answered smilingly—

" Sir page, I pray your grace !
    Certes, I meant not so
To cross your pastoral mood, sir page,
    With the crook of the battle-bow ;
But a knight may speak of a lady's face,
I ween, in any mood or place,
    If the grasses die or grow.

" And this I meant to say —
    My lady's face shall shine
As ladies' faces use, to greet
    My page from Palestine ;
Or, speak she fair or prank she gay,
    She is no lady of mine.

" And this I meant to fear—
    Her bower may suit thee ill ;
For, sooth, in that same field and tent,
    Thy *talk* was somewhat still :
And fitter thy hand for my knightly spear
    Than thy tongue for my lady's will ! "

Slowly and thankfully
  The young page bowed his head ;
His large eyes seemed to muse a smile,
  Until he blushed instead,
And no lady in her bower, pardiè,
  Could blush more sudden red :
" Sir knight,—thy lady's bower to me
  Is suited well," he said.

Beati, beati, mortui !
From the convent on the sea,
One mile off, or scarce so nigh,
Swells the dirge as clear and high
As if that, over brake and lea,
Bodily the wind did carry
The great altar of St Mary,
And the fifty tapers burning o'er it,
And the Lady Abbess dead before it,
And the chanting nuns whom yesterweek
Her voice did charge and bless,—
Chanting steady, chanting meek,
Chanting with a solemn breath,
Because that they are thinking less
Upon the dead than upon death.
Beati, beati, mortui !
Now the vision in the sound
Wheeleth on the wind around ;
Now it sweepeth back, away—
The uplands will not let it stay

To dark the western sun :
Mortui !— away at last,—
Or ere the page's blush is past !
And the knight heard all, and the page heard
    none.

" A boon, thou noble knight,
    If ever I servëd thee !
Though thou art a knight and I am a page,
    Now grant a boon to me ;
And tell me sooth, if dark or bright,
If little loved or loved aright
    Be the face of thy ladye."

Gloomily looked the knight—
    " As a son thou hast servëd me,
And would to none I had granted boon
    Except to only thee !
For haply then I should love aright,
For then I should know if dark or bright
    Were the face of my ladye.

" Yet it ill suits my knightly tongue
    To grudge that granted boon,
That heavy price from heart and life
    I paid in silence down ;
The hand that claimed it, cleared in fine
My father's fame : I swear by mine,
    That price was nobly won !

" Earl Walter was a brave old earl,
　He was my father's friend ;
And while I rode the lists at court
　And little guessed the end,
My noble father in his shroud
Against a slanderer lying loud,
　He rose up to defend.

" Oh, calm below the marble grey
　My father's dust was strown !
Oh, meek above the marble grey
　His image prayed alone !
The slanderer lied : the wretch was brave—
For, looking up the minster-nave,
He saw my father's knightly glaive
　Was changed from steel to stone.

" Earl Walter's glaive was steel,
　With a brave old hand to wear it,
And dashed the lie back in the mouth
Which lied against the godly truth
　And against the knightly merit :
The slanderer, 'neath the avenger's heel,
Struck up the dagger in appeal
From stealthy lie to brutal force—
And out upon the traitor's corse
　Was yielded the true spirit.

" I would mine hand had fought that fight
　And justified my father !

I would mine heart had caught that wound
   And slept beside him rather!
I think it were a better thing
Than murdered friend and marriage-ring
   Forced on my life together.

" Wail shook Earl Walter's house ;
   His true wife shed no tear ;
She lay upon her bed as mute
   As the earl did on his bier :
Till—' Ride, ride fast,' she said at last,
   ' And bring the avengëd's son anear!
Ride fast, ride free, as a dart can flee,
For white of blee with waiting for me
   Is the corse in the next chambere.'

" I came, I knelt beside her bed ;
   Her calm was worse than strife.
' My husband, for thy father dear,
Gave freely when thou wast not here
   His own and eke my life.
A boon ! Of that sweet child we make
An orphan for thy father's sake,
   Make thou, for ours, a wife.'

" I said, ' My steed neighs in the court,
   My bark rocks on the brine,
And the warrior's vow I am under now
   To free the pilgrim's shrine :

But fetch the ring and fetch the priest
  And call that daughter of thine,
And rule she wide from my castle on Nyde
  While I am in Palestine.'

" In the dark chambere, if the bride was fair,
  Ye wis, I could not see,
But the steed thrice neighed, and the priest
    fast prayed,
  And wedded fast were we.
Her mother smiled upon her bed
As at its side we knelt to wed,
  And the bride rose from her knee
And kissed the smile of her mother dead,
  Or ever she kissed me.

" My page, my page, what grieves thee so,
  That the tears run down thy face ? "—
" Alas, alas ! mine own sister
  Was in thy lady's case :
But *she* laid down the silks she wore
And followed him she wed before,
Disguised as his true servitor,
  To the very battle-place."

And wept the page, but laughed the knight,
  A careless laugh laughed he :
" Well done it were for thy sistèr,
  But not for my ladye !

My love, so please you, shall requite
No woman, whether dark or bright,
  Unwomaned if she be."

The page stopped weeping, and smiled cold—
  " Your wisdom may declare
That womanhood is proved the best
By golden brooch and glossy vest
  The mincing ladies wear ;
Yet is it proved, and was of old,
Anear as well, I dare to hold,
  By truth, or by despair."

He smiled no more, he wept no more,
  But passionate he spake—
" Oh, womanly she prayed in tent,
  When none beside did wake !
Oh, womanly she paled in fight,
  For one belovëd's sake !—
And her little hand, defiled with blood,
Her tender tears of womanhood
  Most woman-pure did make ! "

—" Well done it were for thy sistèr,
  Thou tellest well her tale !
But for my lady, she shall pray
  I' the kirk of Nydesdale.
Not dread for me but love for me
  Shall make my lady pale ;

No casque shall hide her woman's tear—
It shall have room to trickle clear
   Behind her woman's veil."

—" But what if she mistook thy mind
   And followed thee to strife,
Then kneeling did entreat thy love
   As Paynims ask for life ? "
—" I would forgive, and evermore
Would love her as my servitor,
   But little as my wife.

" Look up—there is a small bright cloud
   Alone amid the skies !
So high, so pure, and so apart,
   A woman's honour lies."
The page looked up—the cloud was sheen—
A sadder cloud did rush, I ween,
   Betwixt it and his eyes.

Then dimly dropped his eyes away
   From welkin unto hill—
Ha ! who rides there ?—the page is 'ware,
   Though the cry at his heart is still :
And the page seeth all and the knight seeth
   none,
Though banner and spear do fleck the sun,
   And the Saracens ride at will.

He speaketh calm, he speaketh low,—
  " Ride fast, my master, ride,
Or ere within the broadening dark
  The narrow shadows hide."
" Yea, fast, my page, I will do so,
  And keep thou at my side."

" Now nay, now nay, ride on thy way,
  Thy faithful page precede.
For I must loose on saddle-bow
My battle-casque that galls, I trow,
  The shoulder of my steed ;
And I must pray, as I did vow,
  For one in bitter need.

" Ere night I shall be near to thee,—
  Now ride, my master, ride !
Ere night, as parted spirits cleave
To mortals too beloved to leave,
  I shall be at thy side."
The knight smiled free at the fantasy,
  And adown the dell did ride.

Had the knight looked up to the page's face,
  No smile the word had won ;
Had the knight looked up to the page's face,
  I ween he had never gone :
Had the knight looked back to the page's
    geste,
  I ween he had turned anon,

For dread was the woe in the face so young,
And wild was the silent geste that flung
Casque, sword to earth, as the boy down-
    sprung
  And stood—alone, alone.

He clenched his hands as if to hold
  His soul's great agony—
" Have I renounced my womanhood,
  For wifehood unto *thee*,
And is this the last, last look of thine
  That ever I shall see ?

" Yet God thee save, and may'st thou have
  A lady to thy mind,
More woman-proud and half as true
  As one thou leav'st behind !
And God me take with Him to dwell—
For Him I cannot love too well,
  As I have loved my kind."

She looketh up, in earth's despair,
  The hopeful heavens to seek ;
That little cloud still floateth there,
  Whereof her loved did speak :
How bright the little cloud appears !
Her eyelids fall upon the tears,
  And the tears down either cheek.

The tramp of hoof, the flash of steel—
   The Paynims round her coming !
The sound and sight have made her calm,—
   False page, but truthful woman ;
She stands amid them all unmoved :
A heart once broken by the loved
   Is strong to meet the foeman.

" Ho, Christian page ! art keeping sheep,
   From pouring· wine-cups resting ? "—
"I keep my master's noble name,
   For warring, not for feasting ;
And if that here Sir Hubert were,
My master brave, my master dear,
   Ye would not stay the questing."

" Where is thy master, scornful page,
   That we may slay or bind him ? "—
" Now search the lea and search the wood
   And see if ye can find him !
Nathless, as hath been often tried,
Your Paynim heroes faster ride
   Before him than behind him."

" Give smoother answers, lying page,
   Or perish in the lying ! "—
" I trow that if the warrior brand
   Beside my foot, were in my hand,
   'Twere better at replying ! "

They cursed her deep, they smote her low
They cleft her golden ringlets through :
The Loving is the Dying.

She felt the scimitar gleam down,
   And met it from beneath
With smile more bright in victory
   Than any sword from sheath,—
Which flashed across her lip serene,
Most like the spirit-light between
   The darks of life and death.

   Ingemisco, ingemisco !
From the convent on the sea,
Now it sweepeth solemnly,
As over wood and over lea
Bodily the wind did carry
The great altar of St Mary,
And the fifty tapers paling o'er it,
And the Lady Abbess stark before it,
And the weary nuns with hearts that faintly
Beat along their voices saintly—
   Ingemisco, ingemisco !
Dirge for abbess laid in shroud
Sweepeth o'er the shroudless dead,
Page or lady, as we said,
With the dews upon her head,
All as sad if not as loud.

III.O

> *Ingemisco, ingemisco*
> Is ever a lament begun
> By any mourner under sun,
> Which, ere it endeth, suits but *one?*
>   E. B. BROWNING.

LITTLE Ellie sits alone
  'Mid the beeches of a meadow
    By a stream-side on the grass,
And the trees are showering down
  Doubles of their leaves in shadow
    On her shining hair and face.

She has thrown her bonnet by,
  And her feet she has been dipping
    In the shallow water's flow :
Now she holds them nakedly
  In her hands, all sleek and dripping,
    While she rocketh to and fro.

Little Ellie sits alone,
  And the smile she softly uses
    Fills the silence like a speech
While she thinks what shall be done,
  And the sweetest pleasure chooses
    For her future within reach.

Little Ellie in her smile
  Chooses—"I will have a lover,
    Riding on a steed of steeds :
He shall love me without guile,
  And to *him* I will discover
    The swan's nest among the reeds.

"And the steed shall be red-roan,
  And the lover shall be noble,
    With an eye that takes the breath :
And the lute he plays upon
  Shall strike ladies into trouble,
    As his sword strikes men to death.

"And the steed it shall be shod
  All in silver, housed in azure,
    And the mane shall swim the wind ;
And the hoofs along the sod
  Shall flash onward and keep measure,
    Till the shepherds look behind.

"But my lover will not prize
  All the glory that he rides in,
    When he gazes in my face :
He will say, 'O Love, thine eyes
  Build the shrine my soul abides in,
    And I kneel here for thy grace!'

" Then, ay, then he shall kneel low,
  With the red-roan steed anear him
    Which shall seem to understand,
Till I answer, ' Rise and go !
  For the world must love and fear him
    Whom I gift with heart and hand.'

" Then he will arise so pale,
  I shall feel my own lips tremble
    With a *yes* I must not say,
Nathless maiden-brave, ' Farewell,'
  I will utter, and dissemble—
    ' Light to-morrow with to-day !'

" Then he'll ride among the hills
  To the wide world past the river,
    There to put away all wrong ;
To make straight distorted wills,
  And to empty the broad quiver
    Which the wicked bear along.

" Three times shall a young foot-page
  Swim the stream and climb the mountain
    And kneel down beside my feet—
' Lo, my master sends this gage,
  Lady, for thy pity's counting !
    What wilt thou exchange for it ?'

" And the first time I will send
   A white rosebud for a guerdon,
     And the second time, a glove ;
But the third time—I may bend
   From my pride, and answer—' Pardon,
     If he comes to take my love.'

" Then the young foot-page will run,
   Then my lover will ride faster,
     Till he kneeleth at my knee :
' I am a duke's eldest son,
   Thousand serfs do call me master,
     But, O Love, I love but *thee !* '

" He will kiss me on the mouth
   Then, and lead me as a lover
     Through the crowds that praise his
     deeds :
And, when soul-tied by one troth,
   Unto *him* I will discover
     That swan's nest among the reeds."

Little Ellie, with her smile
   Not yet ended, rose up gaily,
     Tied the bonnet, donned the shoe,

And went homeward, round a mile,
  Just to see, as she did daily,
    What more eggs were with the two.

Pushing through the elm-tree copse,
  Winding up the stream, light-hearted,
    Where the osier pathway leads,
Past the boughs she stoops—and stops.
  Lo, the wild swan had deserted,
    And a rat had gnawed the reeds.

Ellie went home sad and slow.
  If she found the lover ever,
    With his red-roan steed of steeds,
Sooth I know not ; but I know
  She could never show him—never,
    That swan's nest among the reeds !
E. B. BROWNING.

≋ The Three Sailors ≋

There were three sailors in Bristol city,
Who took a boat and went to sea.

But first with beef and captains' biscuit,
And pickled pork they loaded she.

There was guzzling Jack and gorging Jimmy,
And the youngest he was little Bil-*ly*.

Now very soon they were so greedy,
They didn't leave not one split pea.

Says guzzling Jack to gorging Jimmy,
I am confounded hung-*ery*.

Says gorging Jim to guzzling Jacky,
We have no wittles, so we must eat *we*.

Says guzzling Jack to gorging Jimmy,
Oh ! gorging Jim, what a fool you be.

There's little Bill as is young and tender,
We're old and tough—so let's eat *he*.

Oh ! Bill, we're going to kill and eat you,
So undo the collar of your chemie.

When Bill he heard this information,
He used his pocket-handkerchee.

Oh ! let me say my catechism,
As my poor mammy taught to me.

Make haste, make haste, says guzzling Jacky,
Whilst Jim pulled out his snicker-snee.

So Bill went up the main top-gallant mast,
When down he fell on his bended knee.

He scarce had said his catechism,
When up he jumps ; " There's land I see !

" There's Jerusalem and Madagascar,
And North and South Ameri-*key*.

" There's the British fleet a-riding at anchor,
With Admiral Napier, K.C.B."

So when they came to the Admiral's vessel,
He hanged fat Jack, and flogged Jim-*my*.

But as for little Bill, he made him
The captain of a Seventy-three.
W. M. THACKERAY.

How they brought the Good
News from Ghent to Aix

16—.

I SPRANG to the stirrup, and Joris, and he ;
I galloped, Dirck galloped, we galloped all three;
" Good speed !" cried the watch, as the gate
bolts undrew,
" Speed !" echoed the wall to us galloping
through ;
Behind shut the postern, the lights sank to rest,
And into the midnight we galloped abreast.

Not a word to each other ; we kept the great
pace
Neck by neck, stride by stride, never changing
our place ;
I turned in my saddle and made its girths tight,
Then shortened each stirrup, and set the pique
right,
Rebuckled the cheek-strap, chained slacker the
bit,
Nor galloped less steadily Roland a whit.

'Twas moonset at starting ; but while we drew
near
Lokeren, the cocks crew and twilight dawned
clear ;

At Boom, a great yellow star came out to see ;
At Duffeld, 'twas morning as plain as could be ;
And from Mecheln church-steeple we heard the
    half-chime,
So, Joris broke silence with, "Yet there is time!"

At Aershot, up leaped of a sudden the sun,
And against him the cattle stood black every one,
To stare thro' the mist at us galloping past,
And I saw my stout galloper Roland at last,
With resolute shoulders, each butting away
The haze, as some bluff river headland its spray:

And his low head and crest, just one sharp ear
    bent back
For my voice, and the other pricked out on his
    track ;
And one eye's black intelligence, — ever that
    glance
O'er its white edge at me, his own master,
    askance !
And the thick heavy spume-flakes which aye
    and anon
His fierce lips shook upwards in galloping on.

By Hasselt, Dirck groaned ; and cried Joris,
    "Stay spur !
Your Roos galloped bravely, the fault's not in
    her,

We'll remember at Aix "—for one heard the
    quick wheeze
Of her chest, saw the stretched neck and
    staggering knees,
And sunk tail, and horrible heave of the flank,
As down on her haunches she shuddered and
    sank.

So, we were left galloping, Joris and I,
Past Looz and past Tongres, no cloud in the
    sky;
The broad sun above laughed a pitiless laugh,
'Neath our feet broke the brittle bright stubble
    like chaff;
Till over by Dalhem a dome-spire sprang white,
And " Gallop," gasped Joris, " for Aix is in
    sight ! "

" How they'll greet us ! "—and all in a moment
    his roan
Rolled neck and croup over, lay dead as a
    stone;
And there was my Roland to bear the whole
    weight
Of the news which alone could save Aix from
    her fate,
With his nostrils like pits full of blood to the
    brim,
And with circles of red for his eye-sockets'
    rim.

Then I cast loose my buffcoat, each holster let
    fall,
Shook off both my jack-boots, let go belt and all,
Stood up in the stirrup, leaned, patted his ear,
Called my Roland his pet-name, my horse with-
    out peer ;
Clapped my hands, laughed and sang, any noise,
    bad or good,
Till at length into Aix Roland galloped and
    stood.

And all I remember is—friends flocking round
As I sat with his head 'twixt my knees on the
    ground ;
And no voice but was praising this Roland of
    mine,
As I poured down his throat our last measure of
    wine,
Which (the burgesses voted by common consent)
Was no more than his due who brought good
    news from Ghent.

R. BROWNING.

≈ Count Gismond ≋

(*Aix in Provence.*)

I.

CHRIST GOD, who savest man, save most
  Of men Count Gismond who saved me !
Count Gauthier, when he chose his post,
  Chose time and place and company
To suit it ; when he struck at length
My honour, 'twas with all his strength.

II.

And doubtlessly, ere he could draw
  All points to one, he must have schemed !
That miserable morning saw
  Few half so happy as I seemed,
While being dressed in queen's array
To give our tourney prize away.

III.

I thought they loved me, did me grace
  To please themselves ; 'twas all their deed ;
God makes, or fair or foul, our face ;
  If showing mine so caused to bleed
My cousins' hearts, they should have dropped
A word, and straight the play had stopped.

IV.

They, too, so beauteous !   Each a queen
   By virtue of her brow and breast ;
Not needing to be crowned, I mean,
   As I do.   E'en when I was dressed,
Had either of them spoke, instead
Of glancing sideways with still head !

V.

But no : they let me laugh, and sing
   My birthday song quite through, adjust
The last rose in my garland, fling
   A last look on the mirror, trust
My arms to each an arm of theirs,
And so descend the castle-stairs—

VI.

And come out on the morning-troop
   Of merry friends who kissed my cheek,
And called me queen, and made me stoop
   Under the canopy—(a streak
That pierced it, of the outside sun,
Powdered with gold its gloom's soft dun)—-

VII.

And they could let me take my state
   And foolish throne amid applause
Of all come there to celebrate
   My queen's-day—Oh I think the cause
Of much was, they forgot no crowd
Makes up for parents in their shroud !

VIII.

However that be, all eyes were bent
  Upon me, when my cousins cast
Theirs down ; 'twas time I should present
  The victor's crown, but . . . there, 'twill last
No long time . . . the old mist again
Blinds me as then it did.   How vain !

IX.

See !   Gismond's at the gate, in talk
  With his two boys : I can proceed.
Well, at that moment, who should stalk
  Forth boldly—to my face, indeed—
But Gauthier ? and he thundered "Stay !"
And all stayed.   " Bring no crowns, I say !

X.

" Bring torches !   Wind the penance-sheet
  About her !   Let her shun the chaste,
Or lay herself before their feet !
  Shall she, whose body I embraced
A night long, queen it in the day ?
For honour's sake no crowns, I say !"

XI.

I ?   What I answered ?   As I live,
  I never fancied such a thing
As answer possible to give.
  What says the body when they spring
Some monstrous torture-engine's whole
Strength on it ?   No more says the soul.

XII.

Till out strode Gismond ; then I knew
   That I was saved.   I never met
His face before, but, at first view,
   I felt quite sure that God had set
Himself to Satan ; who would spend
A minute's mistrust on the end ?

XIII.

He strode to Gauthier, in his throat
   Gave him the lie, then struck his mouth
With one back-handed blow that wrote
   In blood men's verdict there.   North, South,
East, West, I looked.   The lie was dead,
And damned, and truth stood up instead.

XIV.

This glads me most, that I enjoyed
   The heart of the joy, with my content
In watching Gismond unalloyed
   By any doubt of the event :
God took that on him—I was bid
Watch Gismond for my part : I did.

XV.

Did I not watch him while he let
   His armourer just brace his greaves,
Rivet his hauberk, on the fret
   The while !   His foot . . . my memory leaves
No least stamp out, nor how anon
He pulled his ringing gauntlets on.

III.   P

XVI.

And e'en before the trumpet's sound
   Was finished, prone lay the false knight,
Prone as his lie, upon the ground :
   Gismond flew at him, used no sleight
O' the sword, but open-breasted drove,
Cleaving till out the truth he clove.

XVII.

Which done, he dragged him to my feet
   And said, " Here die, but end thy breath
In full confession, lest thou fleet
   From my first, to God's second death !
Say, hast thou lied ? "   And, " I have lied
To God and her," he said, and died.

XVIII.

Then Gismond, kneeling to me, asked
   —What safe my heart holds, though no
      word
Could I repeat now, if I tasked
   My powers for ever, to a third
Dear even as you are.   Pass the rest
Until I sank upon his breast.

XIX.

Over my head his arm he flung
   Against the world ; and scarce I felt

His sword (that dripped by me and swung)
   A little shifted in its belt :
For he began to say the while
How South our home lay many a mile.

XX.

So, 'mid the shouting multitude
   We two walked forth to never more
Return.   My cousins have pursued
   Their life, untroubled as before
I vexed them.   Gauthier's dwelling-place
God lighten !   May his soul find grace.

XXI.

Our elder boy has got the clear
   Great brow ; tho' when his brother's black
Full eye shows scorn, it . . . Gismond here ?
   And have you brought my tercel back ?
I just was telling Adela
How many birds it struck since May.

R. BROWNING.

≋ A Lowland Witch Ballad ≋

THE old witch-wife beside her door
   Sat spinning with a watchful ear,
A horse's hoof upon the road
   Is what she waits for, longs to hear.

The mottled gloaming dusky grew,
  Or else we might a furrow trace,
Sowed with small bones and leaves of yew,
  Across the road from place to place.

Hark he comes! The young bridegroom,
  Singing gaily down the hill,
Rides on, rides blindly to his doom,
  His heart that witch hath sworn to kill.

Up to the fosse he rode so free,
  There his steed stumbled and he fell,
He cannot pass, nor turn, nor flee ;
  His song is done, he's in the spell.

She dances round him where he stands,
  Her distaff touches both his feet,
She blows upon his eyes and hands,
  He has no power his fate to cheat.

" Ye cannot visit her to-night,
  Nor ever again," the witch-wife cried ;
" But thou shalt do as I think right,
  And do it swift without a guide.

" Upon the top of Tintock Hill
  This night there rests the yearly mist,
In silence go, your tongue keep still,
  And find for me the dead man's kist.

"Within the kist there is a cup,
  Thou'lt find it by the dead man's shine,
Take it thus! thus fold it up,—
  It holds for me the wisdom-wine.

"Go to the top of Tintock hill,
  Grope within that eerie mist,
Whatever happens, keep quite still
  Until ye find the dead man's kist.

"The kist will open, take the cup,
  Heed ye not the dead man's shine,
Take it thus, thus fold it up,
  Bring it to me and I am thine."

He went, he could make answer none,
  He went, he found all as she said,
Before the dawn had well begun
  She had the cup from that strange bed.

Into the hut she fled at once,
  She drank the wine ;—forthwith behold !
A radiant damozel advance
  From that black door in silken fold.

The little Circe flower she held
  Towards the boy with such a smile
Made his heart leap, he was compelled
  To take it gently as a child.

She turned, he followed, passed the door,
Which closed behind : at noon next day,
Ambling on his mule that way,
The Abbot found the steed, no more,
The rest was lost in glamoury.

WILLIAM BELL SCOTT.

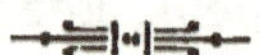

The Weird Lady

THE swevens came up round Harold the Earl,
    Like motes in the sunnès beam ;
And over him stood the Weird Lady,
In her charmèd castle over the sea,
    Sang " Lie thou still and dream."

" Thy steéd is dead in his stall, Earl Harold,
    Since thou hast been with me ;
The rust has eaten thy harness bright,
And the rats have eaten thy greyhound light,
    That was so fair and free."

Mary Mother she stooped from heaven ;
She wakened Earl Harold out of his sweven,
    To don his harness on ;
And over the land and over the sea
He wended abroad to his own countrie,
    A weary way to gon.

Oh but his beard was white with eld,
　　Oh but his hair was gray ;
He stumbled on by stock and stone,
And as he journeyed he made his moan
　　Along that weary way.

Earl Harold came to his castle wall ;
　　The gate was burnt with fire ;
Roof and rafter were fallen down,
The folk were strangers all in the town,
　　And strangers all in the shire.

Earl Harold came to a house of nuns,
　　And he heard the dead-bell toll ;
He saw the sexton stand by a grave ;
" Now Christ have mercy, who did us save,
　　Upon yon fair nun's soul."

The nuns they came from the convent gate
　　By one, by two, by three ;
They sang for the soul of a lady bright
Who died for the love of a traitor knight :
　　It was his own lady.

He stayed the corpse beside the grave ;
　　" A sign, a sign !" quod he.
" Mary Mother who rulest heaven,
Send me a sign if I be forgiven
　　By the woman who so loved me."

A white dove out of the coffin flew ;
　Earl Harold's mouth it kist ;
He fell on his face, wherever he stood ;
And the white dove carried his soul to God
　Or ever the bearers wist.

C. KINGSLEY.

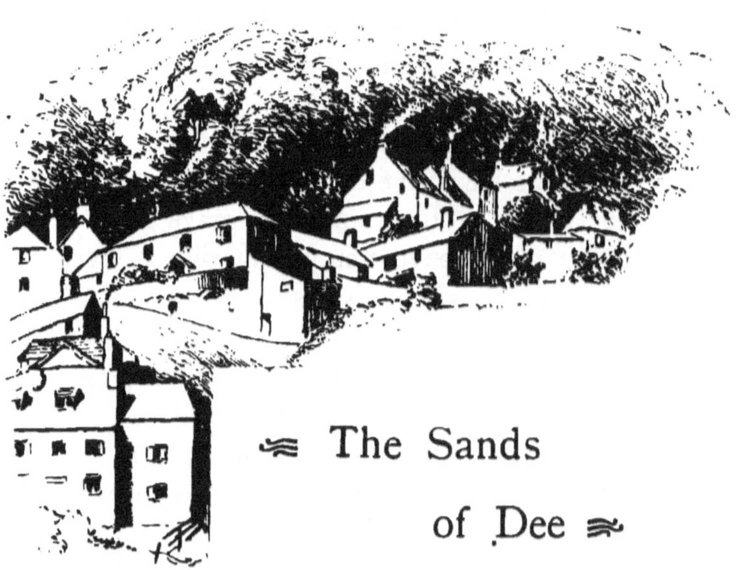

≋ The Sands

of Dee ≋

"O MARY, go and call the cattle home,
　And call the cattle home,
　And call the cattle home
　Across the sands of Dee ; "
The western wind was wild and dank with foam,
And all alone went she.

The western tide crept up along the sand,
   And o'er and o'er the sand,
   And round and round the sand,
  As far as eye could see.
The rolling mist came down and hid the land :
  And never home came she.

" Oh ! is it weed, or fish, or floating hair—
   A tress of golden hair,
   A drownèd maiden's hair
  Above the nets at sea ?
Was never salmon yet that shone so fair
  Among the stakes on Dee."

They rowed her in across the rolling foam,
   The cruel crawling foam,
   The cruel hungry foam,
  To her grave beside the sea :
But still the boatmen hear her call the cattle home
  Across the sands of Dee.

C. KINGSLEY.

≋ Ballad of Earl
Haldan's Daughter ≋

It was Earl Haldan's daughter,
  She looked across the sea ;
She looked across the water ;
  And long and loud laughed she :

" The locks of six princesses
　　Must be my marriage fee,
So hey bonny boat, and ho bonny boat !
　　Who comes a wooing me ? "

It was Earl Haldan's daughter,
　　She walked along the sand ;
When she was aware of a knight so fair,
　　Came sailing to the land.
His sails were all of velvet,
　　His mast of beaten gold,
And " Hey bonny boat, and ho bonny boat !
　　Who saileth here so bold ? "

" The locks of five princesses
　　I won beyond the sea ;
I clipt their golden tresses,
　　To fringe a cloak for thee.
One handful yet is wanting,
　　But one of all the tale ;
So hey bonny boat, and ho bonny boat !
　　Furl up thy velvet sail ! "

He leapt into the water,
　　That rover young and bold ;
He gript Earl Haldan's daughter,
　　He clipt her locks of gold :
" Go weep, go weep, proud maiden,
　　The tale is full to-day.
Now hey bonny boat, and ho bonny boat !
　　Sail Westward ho ! away ! "
C. KINGSLEY.

≈ Lorraine, Lorraine, Lorrèe ≈

I.

" ARE you ready for your steeple-chase, Lorraine,
　　Lorraine, Lorrèe ?
　　　　Barum, Barum, Barum, Barum, Barum,
　　　　Barum, Baree,
You're booked to ride your capping race to-day
　　at Coulterlee,
You're booked to ride Vindictive, for all the
　　world to see,
To keep him straight, to keep him first, and
　　win the run for me.
　　　　Barum, Barum," etc.

II.

She clasped her new-born baby, poor Lorraine,
　　Lorraine, Lorrèe,
" I cannot ride Vindictive, as any man might see,
And I will not ride Vindictive, with this baby
　　on my knee ;
He's killed a boy, he's killed a man, and why
　　must he kill me ? "

III.

" Unless you ride Vindictive, Lorraine, Lorraine,
　　Lorrèe,
Unless you ride Vindictive to-day at Coulterlee,

And land him safe across the brook, and win the
    blank for me,
It's you may keep your baby, for you'll get no
    keep from me."

IV.

" That husbands could be cruel," said Lorraine,
    Lorraine, Lorrèe,
" That husbands could be cruel, I have known
    for seasons three ;
But oh ! to ride Vindictive while a baby cries
    for me,
And be killed across a fence at last for all the
    world to see ! "

V.

She mastered young Vindictive—Oh ! the gallant
    lass was she,
And kept him straight and won the race as near
    as near could be ;
But he killed her at the brook against a pollard
    willow-tree,
Oh ! he killed her at the brook, the brute, for
    all the world to see,
And no one but the baby cried for poor Lorraine,
    Lorrèe.

C. Kingsley.

≋ A Ballad for a Boy ≋

WHEN George the Third was reigning a hundred
  years ago,
He ordered Captain Farmer to chase the foreign
  foe.
" You're not afraid of shot," said he, " you're
  not afraid of wreck,
So cruise about the west of France in the frigate
  called *Quebec*.

" Quebec was once a Frenchman's town, but
  twenty years ago
King George the Second sent a man called
  General Wolfe, you know,
To clamber up a precipice and look into Quebec,
As you'd look down a hatchway when standing
  on the deck.

" If Wolfe could beat the Frenchmen then so
  you can beat them now.
Before he got inside the town he died, I must
  allow.
But since the town was won for us it is a lucky
  name,
And you'll remember Wolfe's good work, and
  you shall do the same."

Then Farmer said, " I'll try, sir," and Farmer
    bowed so low
That George could see his pigtail tied in a velvet
    bow.
George gave him his commission, and that it
    might be safer,
Signed " King of Britain, King of France," and
    sealed it with a wafer.

Then proud was Captain Farmer in a frigate of
    his own,
And grander on his quarter-deck than George
    upon the throne.
He'd two guns in his cabin, and on the spar-deck
    ten,
And twenty on the gun-deck, and more than ten
    score men.

And as a huntsman scours the brakes with six-
    teen brace of dogs,
With two-and-thirty cannon the ship explored
    the fogs.
From Cape la Hogue to Ushant, from Roche-
    forte to Belleisle,
She hunted game till reef and mud were rubbing
    on her keel.

The fogs are dried, the frigate's side is bright
    with melting tar,
The lad up in the foretop sees square white sails
    afar ;

The east wind drives three square-sailed masts
    from out the Breton bay,
And "Clear for action!" Farmer shouts, and
    reefers yell "Hooray!"

The Frenchmen's captain had a name I wish I
    could pronounce ;
A Breton gentleman was he, and wholly free
    from bounce,
One like those famous fellows who died by guil-
    lotine
For honour and the fleurs-de-lys, and Antoinette
    the Queen.

The Catholic for Louis, the Protestant for George,
Each captain drew as bright a sword as saintly
    smiths could forge ;
And both were simple seamen, but both could
    understand
How each was bound to win or die for flag and
    native land.

The French ship was *la Surveillante*, which means
    the watchful maid ;
She folded up her head-dress and began to
    cannonade.
Her hull was clean, and ours was foul ; we had
    to spread more sail.
On canvas, stays, and topsail yards her bullets
    came like hail.

Sore smitten were both captains, and many lads
    beside,
And still to cut our rigging the foreign gunners
    tried.
A sail-clad spar came flapping down athwart a
    blazing gun ;
We could not quench the rushing flames, and so
    the Frenchman won.

Our quarter-deck was crowded, the waist was
    all aglow ;
Men hung upon the taffrail half scorched, but
    loth to go ;
Our captain sat where once he stood, and would
    not quit his chair.
He bade his comrades leap for life, and leave
    him bleeding there.

The guns were hushed on either side, the French-
    men lowered boats,
They flung us planks and hencoops, and every-
    thing that floats.
They risked their lives, good fellows ! to bring
    their rivals aid.
'Twas by the conflagration the peace was
    strangely made.

La Surveillante was like a sieve ; the victors had
    no rest.
They had to dodge the east wind to reach the
    port of Brest,

And where the waves leapt lower, and the
    riddled ship went slower,
In triumph, yet in funeral guise, came fisher-
    boats to tow her.

They dealt with us as brethren, they mourned
    for Farmer dead ;
And as the wounded captives passed each Breton
    bowed the head.
Then spoke the French Lieutenant, " 'Twas fire
    that won, not we.
You never struck your flag to us ; you'll go to
    England free."

'Twas the sixth day of October, seventeen
    hundred seventy-nine,
A year when nations ventured against us to
    combine,
Quebec was burnt and Farmer slain, by us re-
    membered not ;
But thanks be to the French book wherein
    they're not forgot.

Now you, if you've to fight the French, my
    youngster, bear in mind
Those seamen of King Louis so chivalrous and kind ;
Think of the Breton gentlemen who took our
    lads to Brest,
And treat some rescued Breton as a comrade and
    a guest.

WILLIAM CORY.

Keith
of
Ravelston

THE murmur of the mourning ghost
  That keeps the shadowy kine ;
'Oh, Keith of Ravelston,
  The sorrows of thy line !'

Ravelston, Ravelston,
  The merry path that leads
Down the golden morning hill
  And through the silver meads ;

Ravelston, Ravelston,
  The stile beneath the tree,
The maid that kept her mother's kine,
  The song that sang she !

She sang her song, she kept her kine,
  She sat beneath the thorn,
When Andrew Keith of Ravelston
  Rode thro' the Monday morn.

His henchmen sing, his hawk-bells ring,
   His belted jewels shine !
Oh, Keith of Ravelston,
   The sorrows of thy line !

Year after year, where Andrew came,
   Comes evening down the glade,
And still there sits a moonshine ghost
   Where sat the sunshine maid.

Her misty hair is faint and fair,
   She keeps the shadowy kine ;
Oh, Keith of Ravelston,
   The sorrows of thy line !

I lay my hand upon the stile,
   The stile is lone and cold ;
The burnie that goes babbling by
   Says nought that can be told.

Yet, stranger ! here, from year to year,
   She keeps her shadowy kine ;
Oh, Keith of Ravelston,
   The sorrows of thy line !

Step out three steps, where Andrew stood —
   Why blanch thy cheeks for fear ?
The ancient stile is not alone,
   'Tis not the burn I hear !

She makes her immemorial moan,
She keeps her shadowy kine ;
Oh, Keith of Ravelston,
The sorrows of thy line !

S. DOBELL.

Daft

Jean

DAFT Jean,
The waesome wean,
She cam' by the cottage, she cam' by the ha',
The laird's ha' o' Wutherstanelaw,
The cottar's cot by the birken shaw ;
An' aye she gret,
To ilk ane she met,
For the trumpet had blawn an' her lad was awa'.

" Black, black," sang she,
" Black, black my weeds shall be,
My love has widowed me !
Black, black ! " sang she.

Daft Jean,
The waesome wean,
She cam' by the cottage, she cam' by the ha',
The laird's ha' o Wutherstanelaw,
The cottar's cot by the birken shaw ;
Nae mair she creepit,
Nae mair she weepit,
She stept 'mang the lasses the queen o' them a',
The queen o' them a',
The queen o' them a',
She stept 'mang the lasses the queen o' them a'.
For the fight it was fought i' the fiel' far awa',
An' claymore in han' for his love an' his lan',
The lad she lo'ed best he was foremost to fa'.

" White, white," sang she,
" White, white, my weeds shall be,
I am no widow," sang she,
" White, white, my wedding shall be,
White, white ! " sang she.

Daft Jean,
The waesome wean,
She gaed na' to cottage, she gaed na' to ha',

But forth she creepit,
While a' the house weepit,
Into the snaw i' the eerie night-fa'.

At morn we found her,
The lammies stood round her,
The snaw was her pillow, her sheet was the snaw;
Pale she was lying,
Singing and dying,
A' for the laddie wha fell far awa'.

" White, white," sang she,
" My love has married me,
White, white, my weeds shall be,
White, white, my wedding shall be,
White, white," sang she !

S. DOBELL.

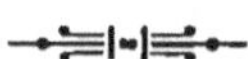

≋ The Yerl o' Waterydeck ≋

THE wind it blew, and the ship it flew,
　　And it was " Hey for hame ! "
But up an' cried the skipper til his crew,
　　" Haud her oot ower the saut sea faem."

Syne up an' spak the angry king :
　　" Haud on for Dumferline ! "
Quo the skipper, " My lord, this maunna be—
　　I'm king on this boat o' mine."

He tuik the helm intil his han' ;
    He left the shore un'er the lee ;
Syne croodit sail, an', east an' south,
    Stude awa' richt oot to sea.

Quo the king, " Leise-majesty, I trow !
    Here lies some ill-set plan.
'Bout ship ! " Quo the skipper, " Yer grace
        forgets
    Ye are king but o' the lan' ! "

Oot he heild to the open sea
    Quhill the north wind flaughtered and fell ;
Syne the east had a bitter word to say
    That waukent a watery hell.

He turned her heid intil the north :
    Quo the nobles: " He's droon, by the mass ! "
Quo the skipper : " Haud aff yer lady-han's,
    Or ye'll never see the Bass."

The king creepit down the cabin-stair
    To drink the gude French wine ;
An' up cam his dochter, the princess fair,
    An' luikit ower the brine.

She turnt her face to the drivin' snaw,
    To the snaw but and the weet ;
It claucht her snood, an' awa' like a clud
    Her hair drave oot i' the sleet.

She turnt her face frae the drivin' win'—
  " Quhat's that aheid ? " quo' she,
The skipper he threw himsel' frae the win',
  An' he brayt the helm alee.

" Put to yer han', my lady fair !
  Haud up her heid," quo' he ;
" Gin she dinna face the win' a wee mair,
  It's faurweel to you an' me ! "

To the tiller the lady she laid her han',
  An' the ship brayt her cheek to the blast ;
They joukit the berg, but her quarter scraped,
  An' they luikit at ither aghast.

Quo the skipper : " Ye are a lady fair,
  An' a princess gran' to see ;
But war ye a beggar, a man wud sail
  To the hell i' yer company."

She liftit a pale an' a queenly face ;
  Her een flashed, an' syne they swam :
" An' what for no to the hevin ? " she says—
  An' she turnt awa' frae him.

Bot she tuik na her han' frae the gude ship's
    helm
  Till the day begouth to daw ;
An' the skipper he spak, but what was said
  It was said atween them twa.

An' syne the gude ship she lay to,
  Wi' Scotlan' hyne un'er the lee ;
An' the king cam up the cabin-stair,
  Wi' wan face an' bluidshot ee.

Laigh loutit the skipper upo' the deck ;
  " Stan' up, stan' up," quo' the king ;
" Ye're an honest loun—an' beg me a boon
  Quhan ye gie me back this ring."

Lowne blew the win' ; the stars cam oot ;
  The ship turnt frae the north ;
An' or ever the sun was up an' aboot,
  They war intil the firth o' Forth.

Quhan the gude ship hung at the pier-heid,
  And the king stude steady o' the lan'—
" Doon wi' ye, skipper—doon ! " he said,
  " Hoo daur ye afore me stan' ? "

The skipper he loutit on his knee ;
  The king his blade he drew :
Quo the king, " Noo mynt ye to contre me ?—
  I'm aboord *my* vessel noo !

" Gien I hadna been yer verra gude lord
  I wad hae thrawn yer neck !
Bot—ye wha loutit Skipper o' Doon,
  Rise up Yerl o' Waterydeck."

The skipper he rasena : " Yer grace is great ;
　Yer wull it can heize or ding ;
Wi' ae wee word ye hae made me a yerl—
　Wi' anither mak me a king."

" I canna mak ye a king," quo' he,
　" The Lord alane can do that ;
I snowk leise-majesty, my man !
　Quhat the Sathan wad ye be at ? "

Glowert at the skipper the doutsum king,
　Jalousin' aneth his croon ;
Quo' the skipper, " Here is yer grace's ring—
　An' yer dochter is my boon."

The black blude shot intil the king's face—
　He wasna bonny to see :
" The rascal skipper ! he lichtlies oor grace !—
　Gar hang him heigh on yon tree."

Up sprang the skipper an' aboord his ship ;
　Cleikit up a bytin' blade ;
An' hackit at the cable that held her to the
　　pier,
　An' thoucht it maist ower weel made.

The king he blew shill in a siller whustle ;
　An' tramp, tramp, doon the pier,
Cam twenty men on twenty horses,
　Clankin' wi' spur and spear.

At the king's fute fell his dochter fair :
  "His life ye wadna spill ! "
" Ye daur stan' twixt my hert an' my hate ? "
  " I daur, wi' a richt gude will ! "

" Ye was aye to yer faither a thrawart bairn ;
  But, my lady, here stan's the king ;
Luikna *him* i' the angry face,
  A monarch's anither thing."

" I lout to my father for his grace,
  Low on my bendit knee ;
But I stan' an' luik the king i' the face,
  For the skipper is king o' me."

She turnt, she sprang upo' the deck ;
  The cable splashed i' the Forth,
Her wings sae braid the gude ship spread
  And flew east, an' syne flew north.

Now was not this a king's dochter--
  A lady that feared no skaith ?
An' a woman wi' quhilk a man micht sail
  Prood intil the port o' Death ?

G. MACDONALD.

≈ Old Sir Walter ≈

(*A Story of* 1734.)

STOUT Sir Walter was old but hearty :
  A velvet cap on his long grey hair,
A full white rose at his gold-laced button :
  Many were laughing, but none looked gayer.

Such a beast was his jet black hunter,
  Silver-spotted with foam and froth,
Brawny in flank and fiery-blooded,
  Stung by the spur to a curbless wrath !

Gaily blowing his horn, he scrambled
  Over the stone wall four feet two ;
See saw over the old park railing,
  Shaking the thistle-head rich with dew.

A long black face the sour Whig huntsman
  Pulled, when he saw Sir Walter come
Trotting up gay by the oak wood cover.
  Why when he cheered did they all sit dumb?

Why when he flung up his hat and shouted,
  " God save King George!" they bawling cried,
As a Justice, drawing a long-sealed parchment,
  Rode up grim to Sir Walter's side.

" In King George's name, arrest him, lieges !
   This is the villain who fought at Boyne :
He sliced the feather from off my beaver,
   And ran his sword twice into my groin."

Then out whipp'd blades : the horns they
      sounded,
   The field came flocking in thick and fast,
But Sir Walter flogged at the barking rabble,
   And through them all like a whirlwind passed.

" A hundred guineas to seize the traitor ! "
   Cried the Justice, purple and white with rage,
Then such a spurring, whipping, and flogging,
   Was never seen in the strangest age.

The hunter whipped off Spot and Fowler,
   Viper and Fury, and all the pack,
And set them fast, with their red tongues lolling
   And white teeth fix'd, on Sir Walter's track.

Loud on the wind came blast of bugle,
   All together the hounds gave tongue,
They swept like a hail-storm down by the gibbet,
   Where the black rags still in the cold storm
      hung.

The rain cut faces like long whip lashes,
   The wind blew strong in its wayward will,
And powdering fast, the men and horses
   Thundering swept down Frampton Hill.

There half the grooms at last pull'd bridle,
   Swearing 'twould ruin their bits of blood ;
Three Whig rogues flew out of the saddle,
   And two were plumped in the river mud.

Three men stuck to the leading rebel;
   The first was a Whig lord, fat and red,'
The next a yellow-faced lean attorney,
   And the last a Justice, as some one said.

Slap at the fence went old Sir Walter,
   Slap at the ditch by the pollard-tree,
Crash through the hazels, over the water,
   And wherever he went, there went the three.

Into the hill-fence broke Sir Walter,
   Right through the tangle of branch and
      thorns,
Swish'd the rasper up by the windmill,
   In spite of the cries and blowing of horns.

Lines of flames trailed all the scarlet
   Streaming, the dogs half a mile before,
Whoop ! with a cry all after Sir Walter,
   Driving wildly along the shore.

Over the timber flew old Sir Walter,
   Light as a swallow, sure and swift,
For his sturdy arm and his " pull and hustle "
   Could help a nag at the deadest lift.

Off went his gold-laced hat and bugle,
　　His scarlet cloak he then let fall,
And into the river spurr'd old Sir Walter,
　　Boldly there, in the sight of all.

There was many a sore on back and wither,
　　Many a spur that ran with red,
But none of them caught the stout Sir Walter,
　　Though they counted of horses sixty head.

There was many a fetlock cut and wounded,
　　Many a hock deep lam'd with thorns,
Many a man that two years after
　　Shuddered to hear the sound of horns.

But on the fallow, the long clay fallow,
　　Foundered his black mare, Lilly Lee,
And Sir Walter sat on the tough old saddle,
　　Waiting the coming of all the three.

Never such chase of stag or vermin,
　　Along the park pale, in and out ;
On they thundered, fast over the railing,
　　Driving the fence in splints about.

The first he shot with his long steel pistol,
　　The second he slew with his Irish sword,
The third he threw in the brook, and mounted
　　Quick on the steed of the fat Whig lord.

Then off to the ship at the nearest harbour,
   Gallop'd Sir Walter, sure and fleet.
He died, 'tis true, in an old French garret,
   But his heart went true to the latest beat.

A white rose, stifled and very sickly,
   Pined for air at the window-sill,
But the last fond look of the brave old trooper
   Was fixed on the dying emblem—still,

All alone in the dusky garret,
   He turn'd to the flower with a father's pride,
" God save King James ! " the old man mur-
     mured,
   " God—save—the—King ! " he moaned and
     died.

G. W. Thornbury.

≋ Sister Helen ≋

" Why did you melt your waxen man,
　　　Sister Helen ?
To-day is the third since you began."
" The time was long, yet the time ran,
　　　Little brother."
　　　　　(O Mother, Mary Mother,
Three days to-day, between Hell and Heaven !)

" But if you have done your work aright,
　　　Sister Helen,
You'll let me play, for you said I might."
" Be very still in your play to-night,
　　　Little brother."
　　　　　(O Mother, Mary Mother,
Third night, to-night, between Hell and Heaven !)

III.　　　　　　　R

" You said it must melt ere vesper-bell,
    Sister Helen ;
If now it be molten, all is well."
" Even so,—nay, peace ! you cannot tell,
    Little brother."
        (*O Mother, Mary Mother,*
O what is this, between Hell and Heaven ?)

" Oh the waxen knave was plump to-day,
    Sister Helen ;
How like dead folk he has dropped away !"
" Nay now, of the dead what can you say,
    Little brother ? "
        (*O Mother, Mary Mother,*
What of the dead, between Hell and Heaven ?)

" See, see, the sunken pile of wood,
    Sister Helen,
Shines through the thinned wax red as blood !"
" Nay now, when looked you yet on blood,
    Little brother ? "
        (*O Mother, Mary Mother,*
How pale she is, between Hell and Heaven !)

" Now close your eyes, for they're sick and sore,
    Sister Helen ;
And I'll play without the gallery door."
" Aye, let me rest,—I'll lie on the floor,
    Little brother."
        (*O Mother, Mary Mother,*
What rest to-night, between Hell and Heaven ?)

" Here high up in the balcony,
        Sister Helen,
The moon flies face to face with me."
" Aye, look and say whatever you see,
        Little brother."
            (*O Mother, Mary Mother,*
What sight to-night, between Hell and Heaven?)

" Outside it's merry in the wind's wake,
        Sister Helen ;
In the shaken trees the chill stars shake."
" Hush, heard you a horse-tread as you spake,
        Little brother."
            (*O Mother, Mary Mother,*
What sound to-night, between Hell and Heaven?)

" I hear a horse-tread, and I see,
        Sister Helen,
Three horsemen that ride terribly."
" Little brother, whence come the three,
        Little brother ? "
            (*O Mother, Mary Mother,*
Whence should they come, between Hell and Heaven ?)

" They come by the hill-verge from Boyne Bar,
        Sister Helen,
And one draws nigh, but two are afar."
" Look, look, do you know them who they are,
        Little brother ? "
            (*O Mother, Mary Mother,*
Who should they be, between Hell and Heaven ?)

" Oh, it's Keith of Eastholm rides so fast,
          Sister Helen,
For I know the white mane on the blast."
" The hour has come, has come at last,
          Little brother ! "
          (*O Mother, Mary Mother,*
Her hour at last, between Hell and Heaven !)

" He has made a sign and called Halloo !
          Sister Helen,
And he says that he would speak with you."
" Oh, tell him I fear the frozen dew,
          Little brother."
          (*O Mother, Mary Mother,*
Why laughs she thus, between Hell and Heaven ?)

" The wind is loud, but I hear him cry,
          Sister Helen,
That Keith of Ewern's like to die."
" And he and thou, and thou and I,
          Little brother."
          (*O Mother, Mary Mother,*
And they and we, between Hell and Heaven !)

" Three days ago, on his marriage-morn,
          Sister Helen,
He sickened, and lies since then forlorn."
" For bridegroom's side is the bride a thorn,
          Little brother."
          (*O Mother, Mary Mother,*
Cold bridal cheer, between Hell and Heaven !)

" Three days and nights he has lain abed,
        Sister Helen,
And he prays in torment to be dead."
" The thing may chance, if he have prayed,
        Little brother."
            (*O Mother, Mary Mother,*
If he have prayed, between Hell and Heaven !)

" But he has not ceased to cry to-day,
        Sister Helen,
That you should take your curse away."
" *My* prayer was heard,—he need but pray,
        Little brother !"
            (*O Mother, Mary Mother,*
Shall God not hear, between Hell and Heaven ?)

" But he says, till you take back your ban,
        Sister Helen,
His soul would pass, yet never can."
" Nay then, shall I slay a living man,
        Little brother ?"
            (*O Mother, Mary Mother,*
A living soul, between Hell and Heaven !)

" But he calls for ever on your name,
        Sister Helen,
And says that he melts before a flame."
" My heart for his pleasure fared the same,
        Little brother."
            (*O Mother, Mary Mother,*
Fire at the heart, between Hell and Heaven !)

" Here's Keith of Westholm riding fast,
          Sister Helen,
For I know the white plume on the blast."
" The hour, the sweet hour I forecast,
          Little brother ! "
          (*O Mother, Mary Mother,*
Is the hour sweet, between Hell and Heaven?)

" He stops to speak, and he stills his horse,
          Sister Helen ;
But his words are drowned in the wind's course."
" Nay hear, nay hear, you must hear perforce,
          Little brother ! "
          (*O Mother, Mary Mother,*
What word now heard, between Hell and Heaven?)

" Oh he says that Keith of Ewern's cry,
          Sister Helen,
Is ever to see you ere he die."
" In all that his soul sees, there am I,
          Little brother ! "
          (*O Mother, Mary Mother,*
The soul's one sight, between Hell and Heaven !)

" He sends a ring and a broken coin,
          Sister Helen,
And bids you mind the banks of Boyne."
" What else he broke will he ever join,
          Little brother ? "
          (*O Mother, Mary Mother,*
No, never joined, between Hell and Heaven !)

" He yields you these and craves full fain,
        Sister Helen,
You pardon him in his mortal pain."
" What else he took will he give again,
        Little brother ?"
            (*O Mother, Mary Mother,*
Not twice to give, between Hell and Heaven !)

" He calls your name in an agony,
        Sister Helen,
That even dead Love must weep to see."
" Hate, born of Love, is blind as he,
        Little brother ! "
            (*O Mother, Mary Mother,*
Love turned to hate, between Hell and Heaven.!)

" Oh it's Keith of Keith now that rides fast,
        Sister Helen,
For I know the white hair on the blast."
" The short short hour will soon be past,
        Little brother ! "
            (*O Mother, Mary Mother,*
Will soon be past, between Hell and Heaven !)

" He looks at me and he tries to speak,
        Sister Helen,
But oh ! his voice is sad and weak ! "
" What here should the mighty Baron seek,
        Little brother ?"
            (*O Mother, Mary Mother,*
Is this the end, between Hell and Heaven ?)

" Oh his son still cries, if you forgive,
      Sister Helen,
The body dies but the soul shall live."
" Fire shall forgive me as I forgive,
      Little brother ! "
        (O Mother, Mary Mother,
As she forgives, between Hell and Heaven !)

" Oh he prays you, as his heart would rive,
      Sister Helen,
To save his dear son's soul alive."
" Fire cannot slay it, it shall thrive,
      Little brother ! "
        (O Mother, Mary Mother,
Alas, alas, between Hell and Heaven !)

" He cries to you, kneeling in the road,
      Sister Helen,
To go with him for the love of God ! "
" The way is long to his son's abode,
      Little brother."
        (O Mother, Mary Mother,
The way is long, between Hell and Heaven !)

" A lady's here, by a dark steed brought,
      Sister Helen,
So darkly clad, I saw her not."
" See her now or never see aught,
      Little brother ! "
        (O Mother, Mary Mother,
What more to see, between Hell and Heaven ?)

"Her hood falls back, and the moon shines fair,
       Sister Helen,
On the Lady of Ewern's golden hair."
" Blest hour of my power and her despair,
       Little brother ! "
         (O Mother, Mary Mother,
Hour blest and bann'd, between Hell and Heaven !)

"Pale, pale her cheeks, that in pride did glow,
       Sister Helen,
'Neath the bridal-wreath three days ago."
" One morn for pride and three days for woe,
       Little brother."
         (O Mother, Mary Mother
Three days, three nights, between Hell and Heaven !)

"Her clasped hands stretch from her bending head,
       Sister Helen ;
With the loud wind's wail her sobs are wed."
" What wedding-strains hath her bridal-bed,
       Little brother ? "
         (O Mother, Mary Mother,
What strain but death's, between Hell and Heaven !)

" She may not speak, she sinks in a swoon,
       Sister Helen,—
She lifts her lips and gasps on the moon."
" Oh ! might I but hear her soul's blithe tune,
       Little brother ! "
         (O Mother, Mary Mother,
Her woe's dumb cry, between Hell and Heaven !)

" They've caught her to Westholm's saddle-bow,
        Sister Helen,
And her moonlit hair gleams white in its flow."
" Let it turn whiter than winter snow,
        Little brother ! "
                (*O Mother, Mary Mother,*
Woe-withered gold, between Hell and Heaven !)

" O Sister Helen, you heard the bell,
        Sister Helen !
More loud than the vesper-chime it fell."
" No vesper-chime, but a dying-knell,
        Little brother ! "
                (*O Mother, Mary Mother,*
His dying knell, between Hell and Heaven !)

" Alas ! but I fear the heavy sound,
        Sister Helen ;
Is it in the sky or in the ground ? "
" Say, have they turned their horses round,
        Little brother ? "
                (*O Mother, Mary Mother,*
What would she more, between Hell and Heaven ?)

" They have raised the old man from his knee,
        Sister Helen,
And they ride in silence hastily."
" More fast the naked soul doth flee,
        Little brother ! "
                (*O Mother, Mary Mother,*   .
The naked soul, between Hell and Heaven !)

"Flank to flank are the three steeds gone,
　　　Sister Helen,
But the lady's dark steed goes alone."
"And lonely her bridegroom's soul hath flown,
　　　Little brother."
　　　　　(*O Mother, Mary Mother,*
The lonely ghost, between Hell and Heaven !)

"Oh the wind is sad in the iron chill,
　　　Sister Helen,
And weary sad they look by the hill."
"But he and I are sadder still,
　　　Little brother !"
　　　　　(*O Mother, Mary Mother,*
Most sad of all, between Hell and Heaven !)

"See, see, the wax has dropped from its place,
　　　Sister Helen,
And the flames are winning up apace !"
"Yet here they burn but for a space,
　　　Little brother !"
　　　　　(*O Mother, Mary Mother,*
Here for a space, between Hell and Heaven !)

"Ah! what white thing at the door has cross'd,
　　　Sister Helen?
Ah! what is this that sighs in the frost?"
"A soul that's lost as mine is lost,
　　　Little brother !"
　　　　　(*O Mother, Mary Mother,*
Lost, lost, all lost, between Hell and Heaven !)
　　　　　　　　　　D. G. ROSSETTI.

The Blackbird's Song

Magdalen at Michael's gate
  Tirled at the pin ;
On Joseph's thorn, sang the blackbird,
  "Let her in ! let her in ! "

"Hast thou seen the wounds ?" said Michael,
  "Know'st thou thy sin ?"
"It is evening, evening," sang the blackbird,
  "Let her in ! let her in ! "

"Yes I have seen the wounds,
  And I know my sin."
"She knows it well, well, well," sang the
    blackbird,
  "Let her in ! let her in ! "

"Thou bringest no offerings," said Michael,
  "Nought save sin."
And the blackbird sang, "She is sorry, sorry,
    sorry,
Let her in ! let her in ! "

When he had sung himself to sleep,
  And night did begin,
One came and opened Michael's gate,
  And Magdalen went in.

H. Kingsley.

≈ Maiden-Song ≈

Long ago and long ago,
    And long ago still,
There dwelt three merry maidens
    Upon a distant hill.
One was tall Meggan,
    And one was dainty May,
But one was fair Margaret,
    More fair than I can say,
Long ago and long ago.

When Meggan plucked the thorny rose,
    And when May pulled the brier,
Half the birds would swoop to see,
    Half the beasts draw nigher ;
Half the fishes of the streams
    Would dart up to admire :
And when Margaret plucked a flag-flower,
    Or poppy hot aflame,
All the beasts, and all the birds,
    And all the fishes came
To her hand more soft than snow.

Strawberry leaves and May-dew
    In brisk morning air,
Strawberry leaves and May-dew
    Make maidens fair.

"I go for strawberry leaves,"
  Meggan said one day :
"Fair Margaret can bide at home,
  But you come with me, May ;
Up the hill and down the hill,
  Along the winding way
You and I are used to go."

So these two fair sisters
  Went with innocent will
Up the hill and down again,
  And round the homestead hill :
While the fairest sat at home,
  Margaret like a queen,
Like a blush-rose, like the moon
  In her heavenly sheen,
Fragrant-breathed as milky cow
  Or field of blossoming bean,
Graceful as an ivy bough
  Born to cling and lean ;
Thus she sat to sing and sew.

When she raised her lustrous eyes
  A beast peeped at the door ;
When she downward cast her eyes
  A fish gasped on the floor ;
When she turned away her eyes
  A bird perched on the sill,
Warbling out its heart of love,
  Warbling warbling still,
With pathetic pleadings low.

Light-foot May with Meggan
  Sought the choicest spot,
Clothed with thyme-alternate grass :
  Then, while day waxed hot,
Sat at ease to play and rest,
  A gracious rest and play ;
The loveliest maidens near or far,
  When Margaret was away,
Who sat at home to sing and sew.

Sun-glow flushed their comely cheeks,
  Wind-play tossed their hair,
Creeping things among the grass
  Stroked them here and there ;
Meggan piped a merry note,
  A fitful wayward lay,
While shrill as birds on topmost twig
  Piped merry May ;
Honey-smooth the double flow.

Sped a herdsman from the vale,
  Mounting like a flame,
All on fire to hear and see,
  With floating locks he came.
Looked neither north nor south,
  Neither east nor west,
But sat him down at Meggan's feet
  As love-bird on his nest,

And wooed her with a silent awe,
  With trouble not expressed ;
She sang the tears into his eyes,
  The heart out of his breast :
So he loved her, listening so.

She sang the heart out of his breast,
  The words out of his tongue ;
Hand and foot and pulse he paused
  Till her song was sung.
Then he spoke up from his place
  Simple words and true :
" Scanty goods have I to give,
  Scanty skill to woo ;
But I have a will to work,
  And a heart for you :
Bid me stay or bid me go."

Then Meggan mused within herself :
  " Better be first with him,
Than dwell where fairer Margaret sits,
  Who shines my brightness dim,
For ever second where she sits,
  However fair I be.
I will be lady of his love,
  And he shall worship me ;
I will be lady of his herds
  And stoop to his degree,
At home where kids and fatlings grow."

Sped a shepherd from the height
　Headlong down to look,
(White lambs followed, lured by love
　Of their shepherd's crook) :
He turned neither east nor west,
　Neither north nor south,
But knelt right down to May, for love
　Of her sweet-singing mouth ;
Forgot his flocks, his panting flocks
　In parching hill-side drouth ;
Forgot himself for weal or woe.

Trilled her song and swelled her song
　With maiden coy caprice
In a labyrinth of throbs,
　Pauses, cadences ;
Clear-noted as a dropping brook,
　Soft-noted like the bees,
Wild-noted as the shivering wind
　Forlorn through forest trees :
Love-noted like the wood-pigeon
　Who hides herself for love,
Yet cannot keep her secret safe,
　But coos and coos thereof :
Thus the notes rang loud or low.

He hung breathless on her breath ;
　Speechless, who listened well ;
Could not speak or think or wish
　Till silence broke the spell.

III.　　　　　　　　S

Then he spoke, and spread his hands,
  Pointing here and there :
"See my sheep and see the lambs,
  Twin lambs which they bear.
And myself I offer you,
  All my flocks and care,
Your sweet song hath moved me so."

In her fluttered heart young May
  Mused a dubious while,
"If he loves me as he says "—
  Her lips curved with a smile :
"Where Margaret shines like the sun
  I shine but like a moon ;
. If sister Meggan makes her choice
  I can make mine as soon ;
At cockcrow we were sister-maids,
  We may be brides at noon."
Said Meggan, "Yes;" May said not "No."

Fair Margaret stayed alone at home,
  Awhile she sang her song,
Awhile sat silent, then she thought :
  "My sisters loiter long."
That sultry noon had waned away,
  Shadows had waxen great :
"Surely," she thought within herself,
  "My sisters loiter late !"
She rose, and peered out at the door,
  With patient heart to wait,

And heard a distant nightingale
  Complaining of its mate ;
Then down the garden slope she walked,
  Down to the garden gate,
Leaned on the rail and waited so.

The slope was lightened by her eyes
  Like summer lightning fair,
Like rising of the haloed moon
  Lightened her glimmering hair,
While her face lightened like the sun
  Whose dawn is rosy white.
Thus crowned with maiden majesty
  She peered into the night,
Looked up the hill and down the hill,
  To left hand and to right,
Flashing like fire-flies to and fro.

Waiting thus in weariness
  She marked the nightingale
Telling, if any one would heed,
  Its old complaining tale.
Then lifted she her voice and sang,
  Answering the bird :
Then lifted she her voice and sang,
  Such notes were never heard
From any bird when Spring's in blow.

The king of all that country,
  Coursing far, coursing near,
Curbed his amber-bitted steed
  Coursed amain to hear ;

All his princes in his train, .
  Squire, and knight, and peer,
With his crown upon his head,
  His sceptre in his hand,
Down he fell at Margaret's knees
  Lord king of all that land,
To her highness bending low.

Every beast and bird and fish,
  Came mustering to the sound,
Every man and every maid
  From miles of country round :
Meggan on her herdsman's arm,
  With her shepherd, May,
Flocks and herds trooped at their heels
  Along the hill-side way ;
No foot too feeble for the ascent,
  Not any head too grey ;
Some were swift, and none were slow.

So Margaret sang her sisters home
  In their marriage mirth ;
Sang free birds out of the sky,
  Beasts along the earth,
Sang up fishes of the deep—
  All breathing things that move
Sang from far and sang from near
  To her lovely love ;
Sang together friend and foe ;

Sang a golden-bearded king
   Straightway to her feet,
Sang him silent where he knelt
   In eager anguish sweet.
But when the clear voice died away,
   When longest echoes died,
He stood up like a royal man
   And claimed her for his bride.
So three maids were wooed and won
   In a brief May-tide,
Long ago and long ago.

CHRISTINA ROSSETTI.

≈ Love from the North ≈

I HAD a love in soft south land,
   Beloved through April far in May ;
He waited on my lightest breath,
   And never dared to say me nay.

He saddened if my cheer was sad,
   But gay he grew if I was gay ;
We never differed on a hair,
   My yes his yes, my nay his nay.

The wedding hour was come, the aisles
   Were flushed with sun and flowers that day ;
I pacing balanced in my thoughts :
   " It's quite too late to think of nay."—

My bridegroom answered in his turn,
   Myself had almost answered " Yea : "
When through the flashing nave I heard
   A struggle and resounding " Nay."

Bridesmaids and bridegroom shrank in fear,
   But I stood high who stood at bay :
" And if I answer yea, fair sir,
   What man art thou to bar with nay ? "

He was a strong man from the north,
   Light-locked, with eyes of dangerous grey :
" Put yea by for another time
   In which I will not say thee nay."

He took me in his strong white arms,
   He bore me on his horse away
O'er crag, morass, and hair-breadth pass,
   But never asked me yea or nay.

He made me fast with book and bell,
   With links of love he makes me stay ;
Till now I've neither heart nor power
   Nor will nor wish to say him nay.
CHRISTINA ROSSETTI.

Maude
Clare

Out of the church she followed them
    With a lofty step and mien :
His bride was like a village maid,
    Maude Clare was like a queen.

"Son Thomas," his lady mother said,
    With smiles, almost with tears :
"May Nell and you but live as true
    As we have done for years ;

"Your father thirty years ago
    Had just your tale to tell ;
But he was not so pale as you,
    Nor I so pale as Nell."

My lord was pale with inward strife,
    And Nell was pale with pride ;
My lord gazed long on pale Maude Clare
    Or ever he kissed the bride.

" Lo, I have brought my gift, my lord,
    Have brought my gift," she said :
" To bless the hearth, to bless the board,
    To bless the marriage-bed.

" Here's my half of the golden chain
    You wore about your neck,
That day we waded ankle-deep
    For lilies in the beck :

" Here's my half of the faded leaves
    We plucked from budding bough,
With feet among the lily leaves,—
    The lilies are budding now."

He strove to match her scorn with scorn,
    He faltered in his place ;
"Lady," he said,—"Maude Clare," he said,—
    " Maude Clare : "—and hid his face.

She turn'd to Nell : " My Lady Nell,
    I have a gift for you ;
Though, were it fruit, the bloom were gone,
    Or, were it flowers, the dew.

" Take my share of a fickle heart,
    Mine of a paltry love :
Take it or leave it as you will,
    I wash my hands thereof."

" And what you leave," said Nell, " I'll take,
    And what you spurn, I'll wear ;
For he's my lord for better and worse,
    And him I love, Maude Clare.

" Yea, though you're taller by the head,
    More wise, and much more fair ;
I'll love him till he loves me best,
    Me best of all, Maude Clare."

CHRISTINA ROSSETTI.

≋ The Seven Fiddlers ≋

A BLUE robe on their shoulder,
  And an ivory bow in hand,
Seven fiddlers came with their fiddles
  A-fiddling through the land,
And they fiddled a tune on their fiddles
  That none could understand.

For none who heard their fiddling
  Might keep his ten toes still,
E'en the cripple threw down his crutches,
  And danced against his will:
Young and old they all fell a-dancing,
  While the fiddlers fiddled their fill.

They fiddled down to the ferry—
  The ferry by Severn-side,
And they stept aboard the ferry,
  None else to row or guide,
And deftly steered the pilot,
  And stoutly the oars they plied.

Then suddenly in the mid-channel
  These fiddlers ceased to row,
And the pilot spake to his fellows
  In a tongue that none may know:
" Let us home to our fathers and brothers,
  And the maidens we love below."

Then the fiddlers seized their fiddles,
  And sang to their fiddles a song :
" We are coming, coming, oh brothers,
  To the home we have left so long,
For the world still loves the fiddler,
  And the fiddler's tune is strong."

Then they stept from out the ferry
  Into the Severn-sea,
Down into the depths of the waters
  Where the homes of the fiddlers be,
And the ferry-boat drifted slowly
  Forth to the ocean free !

But where those jolly fiddlers
  Walked down into the deep,
The ripples are never quiet,
  But for ever dance and leap,
Though the Severn-sea be silent,
  And the winds be all asleep.

SEBASTIAN EVANS.

Sir Nicholas
at Marston Moor

To horse, to horse, Sir Nicholas! the clarion's
    note is high ;
To horse, to horse, Sir Nicholas! the big drum
    makes reply :
Ere this hath Lucas marched with his gallant
    cavaliers,
And the bray of Rupert's trumpets grows
    fainter on our ears.
To horse, to horse, Sir Nicholas! White Guy is
    at the door,
And the vulture whets his beak o'er the field of
    Marston Moor.

Up rose the Lady Alice from her brief and
    broken prayer,
And she brought a silken standard down the
    narrow turret stair.
Oh, many were the tears that those radiant eyes
    had shed,
As she worked the bright word " Glory " in the
    gay and glancing thread ;
And mournful was the smile which o'er those
    beauteous features ran,
As she said, " It is your lady's gift ; unfurl it in
    the van."

" It shall flutter, noble wench, where the best
    and boldest ride,
Through the steel-clad files of Skippon, and the
    black dragoons of Pride ;
The recreant soul of Fairfax will feel a sicklier
    qualm,
And the rebel lips of Oliver give out a louder
    psalm,
When they see my lady's gew-gaw flaunt
    bravely on their wing,
And hear her loyal soldier's shout, For God and
    for the King ! "—

'Tis noon ; the ranks are broken along the
    royal line ;
They fly, the braggarts of the Court, the bullies
    of the Rhine :
Stout Langley's cheer is heard no more, and
    Astley's helm is down,
And Rupert sheathes his rapier with a curse and
    with a frown ;
And cold Newcastle mutters, as he follows in
    the flight,
" The German boar had better far have supped
    in York to-night."

The Knight is all alone, his steel cap cleft in
    twain,
His good buff jerkin crimsoned o'er with many
    a gory stain ;

Yet still he waves the standard, and cries amid
    the rout—
" For Church and King, fair gentlemen, spur
    on and fight it out ! "
And now he wards a Roundhead's pike, and
    now he hums a stave,
And here he quotes a stage-play, and there he
    fells a knave.

Good speed to thee, Sir Nicholas ! thou hast
    no thought of fear ;
Good speed to thee, Sir Nicholas ! but fearful
    odds are here.
The traitors ring thee round, and with every
    blow and thrust,
" Down, down," they cry, " with Belial, down
    with him to the dust ! "
" I would," quoth grim old Oliver, " that
    Belial's trusty sword
This day were doing battle for the Saints and
    for the Lord ! "—

The lady Alice sits with her maidens in her
    bower ;
The grey-haired warden watches on the castle's
    highest tower.—
" What news, what news, old Anthony ? "—
    " The field is lost and won ;
The ranks of war are melting as the mists
    beneath the sun ;

Aud a wounded man speeds hither,—I am old
    and cannot see,
Or sure I am that sturdy step my master's step
    should be ! "—

" I bring thee back the standard from as rude
    and rough a fray,
As e'er was proof of soldier's thews, or theme
    for minstrel's lay.
Bid Hubert fetch the silver bowl, and liquor
    quantum suff.;
I'll make a shift to drain it, ere I part with boot
    and buff;
Though Guy through many a gaping wound is
    breathing out his life,
And I come to thee a landless man, my fond
    and faithful wife !

" Sweet, we will fill our money-bags, and freight
    a ship for France,
And mourn in merry Paris for this poor realm's
    mischance;
Or, if the worst betide me, why, better axe or
    rope,
Than life with Lenthal for a king, and Peters
    for a pope !
Alas, alas, my gallant Guy !—out on the crop-
    eared boor,
That sent me with my standard on foot from
    Marston Moor ! "

W. M. PRAED.

Index to Titles

PRINTED BY
TURNBULL AND SPEARS,
EDINBURGH.

www.ingramcontent.com/pod-product-compliance
Lightning Source LLC
Chambersburg PA
CBHW020927120726
47905CB00008B/2413